D1066829

When Peggy McAllister learns about the Rattletop Award for "excellence in eighth grade social studies," she is determined to win it with a research paper on a Great American Hero. But when she chooses Molly Pitcher, the famous Revolutionary War heroine of the Battle of Monmouth, as her subject, she runs into difficulties.

With the help of her Greatgramps, a retired private investigator, his lady friend Mrs. Spinner, a local historian and secret author of historical romance novels, and Ms. Guelphstein, a dedicated reference librarian, Peggy sorts through a maze of confusing and contradictory evidence to identify the "real" Molly Pitcher.

As Peggy collects sources, evaluates evidence, and traces the twists and turns of the development of folklore, she uncovers the fine line separating fact and fiction and discovers the joys of historical research.

"Linda Grant De Pauw is a skilled historian who takes us on an exciting detective hunt for Molly Pitcher. What a wonderful way for young readers to learn how to separate historical fact from fiction— and have a lot of fun doing it. I loved this book."

—Alfred F. Young, author of *Masquerade: The Life and Times of Deborah Sampson, Continental Soldier*

"De Pauw takes a familiar anecdote from American history, creates a believable cast of modern characters, and weaves a clever story where the protagonist searches high and low to verify the story of Molly Pitcher in the Revolutionary War. Historical method and inquiry, verification of facts, and sifting of information are constant threads that offer the reader useful instruction in the guise of a detective story."

—Eric G. Grundset, Library Director, National Society Daughters of the American Revolution

"As the creator and presenter of a first-person living history program based on the Revolutionary War experience of Mary Hays, I have the unique perspective of having encountered the very same puzzles, frustrations, and decisions as Dr. De Pauw's eighth grade heroine. The author accomplishes the daunting task of revealing the process of historical research on a topic complicated by myths and misinformation in a way that is engaging and accessible to middle school students. *In Search of Molly Pitcher* deserves three huzzahs! "

—Stacy F. Roth, Historical Interpreter, *"Over Here, Molly Pitcher: Stories of a Woman of the Army in the American Revolution"*

"I found Dr. De Pauw's work to be very enjoyable to read and very entertaining. It will sit well with adolescent girls, and boys will be interested in it, too. Her work is good enough to convince a retired field artillery officer that Peggy might be right about our heroine Molly Pitcher."

—LTC Eugene (Gene) P. Moser, Jr. (Ret.), Honorable Order of St. Barbara

"*In Search of Molly Pitcher* should be on all middle school required reading lists. Students will identify with the main character, Peggy, as she researches the little known life of Molly Pitcher. Enjoyable reading for adults, too!"

—Barbara J. Crudale, Docent at Smith's Castle, North Kingstown, Rhode Island; School Counselor, South Kingstown High School; President, Rhode Island School Counselor Association

"*In Search of Molly Pitcher* is a fast-paced book that you will not want to put down. Linda Grant De Pauw follows 8th grader Peggy McAllister while she does research for a school paper. Peggy's topic is Molly Pitcher, and through the course of the book, the reader is treated to a fascinating solution to an historic mystery. As both a re-enactor and an Historian in Residence working with a Teaching American History program, I would recommend this book for students and teachers alike. It clearly points out the difference between primary and secondary sources, clearly walks a student through the process of researching a paper, and does it all in a very entertaining manner. I enjoyed it so much that I read it straight through."

—Beth Gilgun, Deerfield Teachers' Center, Pocumtuck Valley Memorial Association

In Search of Molly Pitcher

OTHER BOOKS BY LINDA GRANT DE PAUW

NON-FICTION

*The Eleventh Pillar: New York State
and the Federal Constitution*

Documentary History of the First Federal Congress

"Remember the Ladies": Women in America 1750-1815

*Battle Cries and Lullabies: Women in War
from Prehistory to the Present*

FICTION

Baptism of Fire

Sea Changes

FOR YOUNG READERS

*Founding Mothers:
Women in the Era of the American Revolution*

Seafaring Women

In Search of Molly Pitcher

Linda Grant De Pauw

Peacock Press of Pasadena

Pasadena, Maryland

Copyright 2007
By Linda Grant De Pauw
All Rights Reserved.

Jacket design and illustration: Kim Jacobs
Book design: Ursa Minor

Library of Congress Control Number: 2007932588

ISBN 978-1-4357-0607-1

Contents

one

The Rattletop Award

As soon as I read about the Rattletop Award in the *Lindwood Weekly News*, I said to myself, "That's mine!" This guy named Richard Rattletop graduated from Lindwood High School way back in 1925. He sure must have gotten teased with a name like that. Or maybe not, because he had, as the story said, "fond memories of his years at Lindwood's fine public schools." Anyway, not surprisingly seeing as he was here that long ago, he died, and in his will he left some money for a prize to be given to a graduating eighth grade student for "excellence in social studies." Every year the Rattletop winner's name would be engraved on a bronze plaque. The name engraved next spring would be the first, and I was determined the name would be Peggy McAllister.

I'm not what you'd call a popular kid. In fact if old Richard Rattletop got teased the way I imagine, I can really relate. I don't work at being weird; it just comes naturally. Of course I don't work at being normal, so maybe I'm asking for it.

I'm not popular, but I am smart. I always get good grades, and being honest, I don't work very hard although I pretend I do. Teachers get mad if they think you're ignoring them, so I have this trick of looking right at the teacher all the time and then going off into my imagination. Keeps everyone happy. If the teacher asks me a direct question, I snap right out of it and always have the right answer. If you think this makes me sound arrogant or stuck up you can see why I am not a popular kid.

Because I read the local paper, I learned about the Rattletop Award in September at the beginning of the school year, and I kept waiting for the social studies teacher, Mr. Pettibone, to say something about it to our class. It was October before he finally got around to it.

Mr. Pettibone is a little man with thinning black hair that he combs across the top of his scalp, and he has a thin black moustache that looks totally ridiculous. Most of the teachers are pretty casual, but Mr. Pettibone always wears a business suit with a vest with a pocket for a watch on a chain. He looks as if he's dressed to be a lawyer in an old movie. He talks that way too.

"Class, pay attention, if you please," he said to us rapping his map pointer on his desk. "The school board has decided on the rules for the Rattletop competition. As some of you may have heard, this is a prize for 'excellence in social studies.' A committee made up of members of the school board and a prominent local historian will decide on the winner. They will judge excellence by your performance on a research paper on a great American hero. Those who compete for the award will work on this project all year and hand in their papers on the last day of classes in May. We will announce the winner at the eighth grade graduation ceremonies."

Except for me, I noticed most of the kids looked bored. Then Mr. Pettibone pulled a dirty trick. "A research paper on a great American hero of your choice will also be an assignment for this class. No one who fails to begin a research paper this term or to submit a completed paper at the last class meeting in May will earn a final grade higher than C." The rest of the students began paying attention.

"What, you may ask, is a research paper and how is it different from an essay or book report?" Mr. Pettibone continued. No one had asked, but that is how he talks. "The difference, class, is summed up in one word: evidence. Research papers are accompanied by what we call 'scholarly apparatus' —a list of the books you read to do the report, known as a bibliography, and footnotes that cite the evidence for every statement in the paper that isn't common knowledge. Today you will select your subjects for this project. Next week you will learn how to assemble a preliminary bibliography."

"What'd he say?" Peter Mitchell, who sits next to me, poked my arm.

"He said pick a subject today and he'll explain the other stuff next week."

"Oh."

Mr. Pettibone handed out a list of Great Americans Everyone Should Know. "Not all of these great Americans qualify as heroes," he said, "but the list gives you a place to start. If anyone strongly objects to choosing from this list," he added looking straight at me, "he or she can select another person with my approval."

I scanned the list. Yeah, I knew them. Lots of presidents and generals. Susan B. Anthony and Neil Armstrong up near the top. Albert Einstein made the list; so did Henry

Ford. I checked to see what women besides Susan B. made Mr. Pettibone's list. I'd heard him mutter about "political correctness" a few times, but he did what was expected of a middle school teacher as we headed into the twenty-first century. Before checking out the women, I noticed that he had put Martin Luther King and George Washington Carver on the list. And Sitting Bull.

I scanned the paper again, from the bottom up this time, looking for women. Sakajawea was there, Harriet Tubman, of course, Eleanor Roosevelt, Pocahontas. And then the name caught my eye that I knew was going to get me the prize: Molly Pitcher.

Now there was a true hero, not a general but a real front lines battlefield type. Plus, I knew less about her than about other people on the list, which meant I could learn something new while I worked on the report and write something the judges hadn't read before. They'd probably be pretty sick of papers about Neil Armstrong, I thought, knowing how the boys in the class were likely to pick the first name they found that looked vaguely exciting.

Mr. Pettibone was impatient to have us make our choices so he could write them down in his book and get on with his scheduled class. Maybe if he had let us take the list home to think about, I would have made another choice. But he didn't.

After only about five minutes, he called us up to his desk one at a time to "discuss" our choice. He called us alphabetically and the "discussion" with all the kids before me was them mumbling a name and him nodding and writing. Then I stood there and said "Molly Pitcher" and ruined his day.

"Peggy," Mr. Pettibone said setting down his pen. "You are a good student and have a chance to win the Rattletop prize if you will take the assignment seriously."

"I am very serious, Mr. Pettibone," I said. "I think I can win the prize with a paper on Molly Pitcher."

Mr. Pettibone sighed. "Molly Pitcher is not a good topic. Too little is known about her. You will find a very short list of books to consult and end up with very few footnotes and a very short paper. The prize doesn't stipulate any minimum length, but I assure you that a seven-page paper with four footnotes won't impress the judges. It won't earn an A grade in this class either."

I get very stubborn when someone tells me there is something I can't do, and Mr. Pettibone brings out the worst in me.

"If there's not enough about Molly Pitcher to do a research paper, why did you put her on the list? It's not like I thought up the topic myself. I just did what you said and picked from the Great Americans list."

"All right, Peggy, all right," Mr. Pettibone said picking up his pen. "I know better than to argue with you. But don't say I didn't warn you. With Susan B. Anthony or Eleanor Roosevelt you would have had a good chance to be the first Rattletop Award winner."

And so, as my Greatgramps would say, the die was cast and I had crossed the Rubicon. For the rest of the school year Molly Pitcher would be at the center of my life.

- two -
Greatgramps

I always go straight home after school except on the days I have band practice. Coming straight home is one of Greatgramps's rules. Actually, I don't mind. It's not like I have any friends to hang out with, and I don't have money to go shopping. Besides, Greatgramps is better than any kid friend I could have. I was eager to tell him about the Rattletop award and how I was going to win.

As usual I found Greatgramps in the kitchen waiting for me with my after school snack. Greatgramps takes good care of me. Mom wouldn't be home before six and might even miss supper if she got overtime hours at Wal-Mart. Greatgramps complains that Mom is too skinny and doesn't eat right, but she is a grownup so he can't do anything about it

Greatgramps sat with his coffee while I drank my milk. We shared a plate of oatmeal cookies laced with wheat germ and other healthy stuff. Greatgramps says that as long as he's become a househusband in his old age, he's going do the job right.

"You're going to write about who?" he asked. "Molly Pitcher? She's not even real. How can you do a research paper on a myth?"

"She is too, real," I said. "She's on Mr. Pettibone's list of Great Americans."

"Oh, now I'm really impressed. The great Mr. Pettibone has spoken."

I sulked. If I hadn't already made such a fuss in school, I would have asked Greatgramps's advice and picked another person, maybe somebody not on the list who was a hero no one had ever heard of.

"What's the matter? Did I insult your prissy little teacher? I didn't think you were such a fan of his."

I snorted into my milk. Greatgramps had a way with words. "Prissy." That was exactly right for Mr. Pettibone. I complained about him all the time. For the first assignment of the year we were supposed to bring in a list of "essential human needs." Mr. Pettibone expected us to write "food, clothing, and shelter." I added oxygen and water and then got to thinking about salt and vitamins like C to prevent scurvy and B to prevent beriberi. I went to the library and talked to the reference librarian and ended up with two pages of stuff. Mr. Pettibone made me do the assignment over so it all fit on one piece of paper and then he only gave me credit for food, clothing, and shelter.

I told Greatgramps how I had cast the die and crossed the Rubicon—and burned my bridges.

"I see," said Greatgramps, brushing cookie crumbs from his moustache. "Then we will have to make the best of it." I grinned. Greatgramps would always back me up.

"Maybe she is real," he said. "And even if she isn't, there might be a real person like her that would do for your project."

"What would I need to have to prove she's real?" Greatgramps was a private investigator before he retired. He knew how to find documents to locate people who were missing or hiding from people who wanted to find them.

"A birth certificate would be good," he said, "a marriage license, military records."

"Yeah," I said. "That's what I want. Military records." I imagined how Mr. Pettibone's weak jaw would drop when I put stuff like that in my bibliography. "How do I get those, Greatgramps?"

"You're getting a little out of my range, Peg. When I was tracking people, I never went looking for someone who'd been dead for two centuries."

My spirits sank. Of course Greatgramps couldn't track down this missing Pitcher person with his usual sources.

"Now, Peg," Greatgramps said. "Just because I can't solve your problem myself, that doesn't mean I can't find someone who can. In fact that's what I'm best at." I cheered up. Greatgramps still has his private investigator business cards that say "solving problems since 1962" and a revolving plastic file full of little cards he calls his "contacts."

"Let's start by analyzing the problem." He reached into the kitchen table drawer and pulled out a lined yellow pad, a pen, and his reading glasses. At the top of the page he wrote "Molly Pitcher" and drew a line dividing the page into two columns. On one side he wrote: "Facts." On the other side he wrote "Questions."

"All right, Peggy. Tell me what you know about Molly Pitcher."

"She was in the Revolutionary War," I said. "At the Battle of Monmouth. Her husband got killed so she took over at the cannon and fired at the enemy."

Greatgramps wrote this down.

"Anything else?"

I tried to remember. I had some hazy idea that George Washington had been involved, that he gave Molly Pitcher a reward, a medal or something, but I didn't really know anything more.

"That's all right, Peg," Greatgramps said. "After all you're just starting your investigation. Now assuming that she is real, what do you want to know about her?"

This was easier. I thought about the kind of information there would be in reports about Neil Armstrong or Susan B. Anthony.

"I want to know when she was born and where, who her parents were, whether she had brothers and sisters. Did she go to school, and if so where? What were her favorite subjects? Did she go to church, if so which one? How did she meet her husband? Why did he decide to join the army, and when did he join? Why did she decide to go with him instead of staying at home? How did she feel about being in the middle of a battle?"

Greatgramps had been scribbling as fast as he could. Now he interrupted me and looked at what he had written.

"If you were writing a novel instead of a research paper, you could answer all these questions, but it probably isn't possible to get this much detail about someone who has been dead for so long. Especially a woman. Until you get to recent times, not many records exist except for important people."

I bristled. "Women were important," I said. "And Molly Pitcher was certainly important. She's famous."

"Well we can try," Greatgramps said. "All you have is her married name. Birth records and school records would be under her maiden name."

"Why don't we start with her husband then?" I said. "What about military records for soldiers named Pitcher? Can you find those? See if there was one who died at the Battle of Monmouth."

"That's a possibility," Greatgramps said. "Let me make some phone calls."

- three -

Mrs. Spinner

Mrs. Spinner knows more about the American Revolution in New Jersey than anyone else in town," Greatgramps said. "She says she is home to visitors Saturday afternoons."

"That's a funny thing to say."

"Yes, it is. So you must be careful not to laugh at her. Mrs. Spinner is an eccentric."

"What's an eccentric?"

"Someone who has found an unusual way to live that suits her and that she sticks to even if other people think she's crazy."

"That's what the kids in school think I am, only they call me weird."

"Exactly. Weird children can grow up to be eccentrics—if they don't sell out." Greatgramps scowled at me, reminding me of his lectures about middle school girls who narrowed their interests to dieting, clothes and boys. Greatgramps thought growing up to be an eccentric was desirable. I wasn't so sure, but I was curious about Mrs. Spinner.

"Mrs. Spinner is descended from one of the oldest families in Lindwood. Her house is on Old Post Road and dates from colonial days. Her family once was wealthy, but these days she has to work to keep the house and pay her bills."

I understood that. Greatgramps's house had belonged to his parents and grandparents. His family was never wealthy, but they once had a lot more than our family does now. Greatgramps owns the house free and clear, so we don't have to pay rent, but we do have to pay taxes and insurance. Since he retired, the only income Greatgramps has comes from his pension and social security, and he needs most of that to pay for his prescriptions. Mom works at her job as many hours as she can get to buy food and the other things we need and to meet the payments on her student loan. I wondered if Mrs. Spinner worked at Wal-Mart. Lots of old women did.

"You must pretend that you don't know, but Mrs. Spinner has an alias." My ears perked up at that. "Alice Spinner is also known as Alicia Spinnaker."

"You mean the author who writes historical romances? The one who wrote *Patriot's Passion* and *Mistress of Monticello*? That is so cool! Wow, just wait 'til I tell the kids at school I've met her."

"Hold on, Peg. You are not going to tell anyone. This is Mrs. Spinner's secret. She is embarrassed about having to work at all. Before she began writing fiction she published *The History of Lindwood* and two biographies of early residents of the town. She wants to be taken seriously as an historian, so she doesn't want it known that she writes novels."

"Well, if that's what she wants," I said. "If I was famous like she is, I would want everyone to know."

"Something else you have to know before we go calling. Mrs. Spinner tries to live as much as she can as people did in the eighteenth century. That's partly because she loves the period and wishes she had lived then and partly because it helps her get in the mood for writing her novels. So I'm telling you again, you must not laugh at her. Get into the spirit of it yourself, if you can. She can help you a lot if she gets to like you."

I folded my hands and nodded solemnly the way I thought a colonial girl might.

"Good," Greatgramps said. "Now we have to dress properly to go calling on Mrs. Spinner. I'm going to wear my sanity hearing suit."

Greatgramps owns only one suit. He gave all the others away after he retired. Greatgramps calls the one he kept his sanity hearing suit because he says if people think you've lost your mind or gone senile and want to lock you up, you have a right to a hearing before a judge just like criminals do. The judge decides if you are sane enough to be out on your own, so Greatgramps says that everyone who wants to act weird from time to time should have one very respectable outfit in the closet for such occasions.

Even though he's old, Greatgramps is handsome when he gets dressed up. He has thick, wavy white hair and a moustache, and when I was small I wanted him to grow a beard so he would look like Santa. Greatgramps said that was the wrong image for a private investigator. He's very tall, over six feet, and he says he used to be even taller. He carries himself straight which he says he learned to do when he was a marine in World War II when he also learned to box and to spit shine his shoes. Greatgramps keeps a pair of spit-shined shoes ready in his closet, and he gave them an extra polish while I got dressed.

I put on what I call my funeral dress because it was bought for a funeral when my grandmother, my Mom's mother, died in Illinois last spring. It's my only dress, but I don't think it would do for a sanity hearing because, in my opinion, it is the weirdest thing I own. It's dark blue with a white top that looks like a blouse and a matching jacket with red cord trim. I looked at myself in the mirror before we left the house. I could be dressed up to look like the Addams kid for Halloween. I didn't mind dressing up for Mrs. Spinner, but I wished I had a colonial costume to wear.

"Shall we go?" Greatgramps said after we had both inspected ourselves one last time in the hall mirror. "It isn't far; we can walk."

Greatgramps has a car, a really neat old Volkswagen that he is always puttering with. The car has what he calls a "souped up" engine, and he says someone would try to steal it if he wasn't so clever about disguising it to look like an old wreck. The engine is better than new, but the body is a mess. Even worse than a mess. Greatgramps decided when the paint first started to peel that repainting would make it look too fancy, so he covered over the bad place with a bumper sticker. He got one free from a political candidate and then worried that someone supporting the other party would bash his car if he used it. So he got a sticker from the other candidate and put both on the car. The paint kept peeling and Greatgramps kept adding stickers, always balancing them. He has a "pro choice" sticker and a "right to life" sticker, a sticker that says "I found Jesus," and one that says "Born Again Pagan." The whole car is covered with these stickers, several layers deep in some places. Greatgramps keeps it waxed and shined. He says he doesn't want to look like a total slob. Anyway, if someone stole it, the cops wouldn't need to check license plates to identify it.

When Greatgramps takes his car out for trips it gets great mileage, but he never takes it out of the garage when he's going less than three miles round trip unless the weather is very bad. He says walking is healthy for people and stop and go driving is bad for cars.

"What about these shoes?" I asked sticking out one of the patent leather party pumps that Mom had bought for me with her discount at Wal-Mart. "Are we going to be taking shortcuts?"

"Yes, we will be, but most of it is on pavement. Don't worry about your shoes; I'm not worried about mine."

We took the short cut through the park, past the library and the police station and the firehouse. Then we took a dirt path through the woods crossing a plank bridge over a creek. Mrs. Spinner was at a spinning wheel by the back door of her house. Greatgramps waved and she nodded. She didn't stop spinning.

"Good afternoon, Mrs. Spinner," Greatgramps said formally. "Allow me to present my greatgranddaughter, Peggy."

"I am pleased to make your acquaintance, Miss Peggy," Mrs. Spinner said. I mumbled something like, "How do you do, likewise I'm sure," wondering if I was supposed to curtsy. I did not laugh although I was tempted. Mrs. Spinner wore a long dress made of some kind of rough brown cloth, a blue gingham apron, and a frilly white cap. Little curly wisps of white hair stuck out at the front. Although she said she was pleased to see me, she didn't look pleased. She looked at me over the top of little half glasses the way the stern old grandmothers did in Alicia Spinnaker's books.

"Please excuse me if I don't offer to shake hands," Mrs. Spinner said. I realized I'd been staring at her hands, but who wouldn't. Mrs. Spinner was spinning fur, her fingers pulling bits from the back of a fat rabbit that sat placidly on her lap.

"You didn't tell me you were bringing a visitor, Mr. McAllister," she said. "I would have changed into something more conventional."

"I'm sorry," Greatgramps said. "I didn't think you'd mind. Don't you still dress this way to visit the schools?"

"I haven't visited the schools for years, Mr. McAllister," Mrs. Spinner said, looking at me. "Children these days are so sophisticated. And they are so restless. They don't know how to sit quietly and watch me work. They make my rabbits nervous."

I didn't know what to say. I looked at the rabbit. It was so relaxed as Mrs. Spinner rhythmically pulled its fur that it seemed barely awake.

"Well my greatgranddaughter doesn't seem to have made this one nervous. Are you feeding him pot?"

"Hah!" Mrs. Spinner barked a laugh. She let the spinning wheel slow and stop and rested both hands on the plump animal. The rabbit looked so soft that I longed to pet it but didn't dare ask.

"I brought Miss Peggy to visit because she is very interested in colonial history, and I thought you could answer some of her questions."

"Really." Mrs. Spinner inspected me more closely.

"Yes, ma'am," I said. "I'm doing a research paper about a woman in the Revolutionary War. Greatgramps says you'd know more about that than anyone else in town."

"Really," Mrs. Spinner said again and smiled at Greatgramps. "Well, Miss Peggy, I've always been happy to assist young scholars who are serious about their studies. Would you hold Fluffy for a moment while I put fresh water in the hutch?" I held out my arms and Mrs. Spinner transferred ten pounds of rabbit that felt like a warm breathing pillow as it rested against me.

Mrs. Spinner shook out her gingham apron and stepped to a pump that she worked vigorously up and down until water spilled into a waiting bucket. She carried it to a row of rabbit hutches and poured drinks for six rabbits all looking as lethargic as Fluffy.

"Thank you, Miss Peggy," she said retrieving Fluffy and putting him into his hutch. "Please allow me to offer you some tea. You do drink tea, I hope, Miss Peggy," she said, glancing at me sharply. "I don't keep a cow."

She led us into her kitchen where a huge fireplace set in the wall facing the door dominated the room. I wondered if Mrs. Spinner would light a fire to boil water. But Mrs. Spinner did allow some of the modern world into her life. She boiled water for tea in an electric kettle just like the one Greatgramps uses.

She served the tea in a room she called her parlor, setting out a silver teapot, a sugar bowl that held lumps of sugar and three china tea cups without saucers on a small piecrust table together with an uncut loaf of bread and a round lump of butter. After a ritual of tea pouring and formal conversation that Greatgramps understood and I kind of imitated, Mrs. Spinner invited me to ask my questions. I took out my list.

"The first thing I need to know is whether there were any soldiers named Pitcher in the Revolutionary War. If there were, I want to know if one of them was married to a woman named Molly."

"Ah, a genealogical inquiry," Mrs. Spinner said putting down her teacup and folding her hands in her lap. "The best resources for genealogical research are the Mormon Church in Utah, the National Archives and my own Daughters of the American Revolution in our nation's capital."

I looked at Greatgramps. He might drive me down to Washington, but Utah was a long way from New Jersey.

"Can I find any sources on a CD?" I asked.

"Or on microfilm?" Greatgramps added.

Mrs. Spinner winced as if she hated to be reminded that such things existed. "I do own some reference books," she said. "I may not be able to tell you about wives, but I can find out if any men named Pitcher were enlisted in the Continental Army. Will that suit your purposes, Miss Peggy?"

I started to say "That would be great!" but I remembered in time and tried to be more colonial. I thought of how the heroines talked in Alicia Spinnaker's novels. "Oh, yes ma'am," I said demurely, "that information would be prized exceedingly."

"Then I will be pleased to assist you, Miss Peggy," Mrs. Spinner said, and this time she did look pleased.

- four -

Mr. Pettibone

On Monday, Mr. Pettibone handed out an assignment sheet with dates for turning in reports to show we were making progress on our research papers. The first assignment was about footnotes and bibliographies.

"Can anyone explain to the class what a footnote is?" My hand shot up. After looking around for another volunteer, Mr. Pettibone called on me.

"A footnote is a note at the bottom of the page in a book that tells where the writer got the information or adds a comment that explains something in more detail."

"We won't be having any comments in our footnotes," Mr. Pettibone said sourly as if he wished my answer had been completely wrong, "but we will be citing sources. A source is evidence."

Peter Mitchell raised his hand. "Is that like when they say on television that an informed source said something without saying who?"

"Yes," said Mr. Pettibone, "that's very good, Peter, but a source is better when the person is named. Then you know how much you can trust the information." Peter beamed.

"Peter has given us an example of a primary source. A primary source is evidence from a person who is an eyewitness to events. A document can be a primary source too. A letter from a soldier who was in a battle is a primary source and so is an article in a newspaper by a reporter who interviewed witnesses. Can anyone give examples of other kinds of primary sources?"

"Birth certificates and military records," I said not waiting to be called on.

Mr. Pettibone nodded impatiently and called on some other waving hands.

"Diaries," someone said.

"Letters."

"Clothing a person wore."

"Sketchbooks."

"Photographs!"

"Tape recordings of phone conversations." This from Dominic Perrizi who had chosen J. Edgar Hoover as his hero.

"Very good," said Mr. Pettibone. "All of these would be listed as primary sources. Most of the sources you will be using, however, are books written by historians who were not actually present to witness the events they describe. Does anyone know what these are called?" I didn't and neither did anyone else which gave Mr. Pettibone the chance to answer his own question.

"They are called secondary sources," he said pressing his fingers together and looking pleased with himself. "Eye witnesses are primary sources. Books written and footnoted to the primary sources are secondary sources."

"Does that mean our research papers will be secondary sources?" Peter asked.

"Perhaps, if anyone else ever cites them in a footnote." Mr. Pettibone took up another stack of papers from his desk and handed them out.

"There is a set style for citing secondary sources in footnotes and bibliographies," he said. "You must follow it exactly or you will be marked down."

I put the style sheet safely away in my notebook together with the assignment sheet. I suspected that Mr. Pettibone didn't even read everything I turned in, but he always noticed spelling and punctuation errors, and he always marked down a full grade for anything that was handed in late.

"Some of you will be unable to locate any primary sources for your subject," he said looking right at me. "But all of you will be using secondary sources, so we will begin with them. You will see that your first research assignment is to find at least three books that might serve as sources for your project. You aren't expected to read them yet; these are books you will examine and make notes from later on this term. For now you are merely to identify the titles and list them in good form under the heading 'Preliminary Bibliography.' This assignment is due a week from Monday."

- five -
The Library

Lindwood, New Jersey is an old town. Some houses still standing were built over three hundred years ago. The original Lindwood Public Library building was built in 1878. The extension was added thirty years ago, a one-story structure that is all bright white walls and glass with computers and displays of all the latest books. Children's books are upstairs in the old building together with storage rooms with shelves of old books that no one takes out any more. Reference books and the local history collection are downstairs, and so is my favorite librarian, Ms. Guelphstein.

I've been coming to the library for as long as I can remember. One of my first memories is getting my library card. To get a card you have to be able to write your name with a pen. I learned to write my name with a pencil when I was two, and Ms. Guelphstein agreed to let me try signing for a library card with her ballpoint pen without being able to erase. She was surprised to see that I could. She laughed, but she gave me the library card. For a few years after that I stayed in the children's room upstairs, but when I was six or seven I started reading grownup books—reading books and asking questions. Ms. Guelphstein still laughed, but she looked up answers for me.

"Hello, Peggy," she greeted me. "Did your teacher agree that education is an essential human need? And did he let you get away with listing all the amino acids?"

"No to both," I said. "But I'm going to get back at him."

"Oh? Nothing violent I hope."

I grinned. I am totally nonviolent. When I think about it, I wonder if it's because I have no choice. I mean, I am not athletic, and if I was attacked it wouldn't do me much good to try to fight back. Probably I wouldn't be able to run fast enough to get away either. If I couldn't talk my way out of trouble, I'd be done for.

"I'm going to win the Rattletop Award," I said. "Did you read about it in the paper? It's for excellence in social studies, and I am going to win by writing a research paper on Molly Pitcher."

"Good for you," Ms. Guelphstein said. "I'll be interested in reading that. I don't know anything about Molly Pitcher except for the cannon and the Battle of Monmouth."

I didn't admit that that was all I knew myself.

"I thought I'd check the library catalog on the computer and see what books you have."

So I did, but I didn't find much. Only four titles came up, and all of them were shelved in the children's room. I climbed the stairs and sat on the floor to look at the books the way I had when I was little.

Two of them were picture books, and the other two were novels. I started with one of the novels called *Molly Pitcher: Girl Patriot*. The author, Augusta Stevenson, said Molly's real name was Mary, but everyone called her Molly. Her name before she got married was Ludwig. Her father was German but her mother was Dutch. Molly was blond like her mother and wore wooden shoes. A Dr. and Mrs. Irvine appeared in the story, and Molly went to work for them. I skimmed through the pages looking for the story of the cannon and the battle of Monmouth, but almost the whole book was about Molly before she was grown up.

Finally, after more than 150 pages, I came to the last chapter, which began, "Twelve years had passed. It was now 1778..." A couple of pages later I found out that Molly had married a man named John, but his last name was Hays, not Pitcher. Finally we got to the Battle of Monmouth where the book said the soldiers gave Mary Ludwig Hays the name Molly Pitcher because she was bringing water to the wounded in a big pewter pitcher. When they wanted a drink they called out "Molly Pitcher."

I closed my eyes and tried to imagine what it would be like to be wounded, to have a terrible pain, maybe in my leg or my stomach, and lying out in the hot sun with blood gushing out. My mouth would be dry, and it would be hard to talk. I imagined pushing myself up on one arm and trying to call out. I'd try to cry, "help!" I thought. If I was really thirsty, I'd moan "water!" I couldn't imagine making the effort to call out "Molly Pitcher." It was harder to say. And how would a soldier even know that the nearest person with water was named Molly and that she was carrying it in a pitcher?

Five pages from the end of the book, we got to the important part: Molly's husband is wounded and all the other soldiers in his gun crew have been killed or wounded. Molly had her heroic moment: "She seized the rammer. She swabbed and loaded and fired," doing the work of the entire gun crew all by herself. The book said she'd learned by watching her husband. She must have been a natural since the orderly said after seeing her fire the first shot, "No gunner could do better," and he left her to work the weapon—swabbing, loading, and firing—all by herself for the rest of the battle.

In the last pages of the book George Washington called for Molly to come to his headquarters and said to her, "We dealt the English a heavy blow. Without your help we might not have succeeded. Therefore, I make you a sergeant in this army. And I now pin this badge of honor upon you." Other generals whose names I recognized put in an appearance—Henry Knox, Nathaniel Greene, and the Marquis de Lafayette. I knew I couldn't trust a novel alone as a source, but if all of these famous people were there and thought what Molly did was so important, at least some of them must have written down eyewitness reports—primary sources.

I took out my social studies notebook and wrote down, "Look for evidence from George Washington, Henry Knox, Nathaniel Greene, and Marquis de Lafayette." I put *Molly Pitcher: Young Patriot* aside and picked up the other novel *A Hatful of Gold* by Marjory Hall.

Hatful of Gold agreed with the first book that the heroine's real name was Mary Ludwig but said both her parents were German, not just her father. She still had golden hair, just like the Dutch girl in the first novel. Mary got her American sounding nickname, Molly, from a girl friend. By the second chapter, Dr. and Mrs. Irvine appear—I made a note that they were probably real and I should check them out. Mary's family sends her away with them to Carlisle, Pennsylvania. Soon she is courted by tall, handsome John Caspar Hays who had an Irish grandmother and loves the name Molly. I had to stop myself from dawdling to read through the courtship scenes. I sternly reminded myself that I had come to the library to do research.

I paged through the book until I found the Battle of Monmouth. Molly has a pitcher she brings to the battlefield. A wounded man tells her where to find a spring to fill it, and when he sees her again he says, "Molly! Please bring your pitcher!" Other soldiers hear him and take up the same call. So, I thought, two books agree on how she got her name though it still seemed improbable to me.

Once again, we had Molly's husband, John Hays, wounded. Only this time one man on the gun crew is still alive and able to work. He can't do the job alone, so Molly had her opportunity:

> Almost without knowing what she was doing, she seized the sponge and soaked it in the bucket, swabbed the gun, then rammed in powder, wadding, and the shot, remembering to match the notches on the rammer as John had told her must be done to make sure each part of the load was seated properly. Those idle lessons, long before, and the relating of what she had learned to John's every move this afternoon made the action seem as normal to her as the churning of butter or the kneading of her dough.

Once again, without any experience, Mrs. Hays is doing the work of most of a gun crew. She does everything but fire the weapon. And when "the man she helped collapsed on the ground ... she tried to do his work too." Naturally others were impressed. "I shall report to General Knox that he has an expert gunner who wears skirts, but who will serve him well," a soldier said.

As in the first book, Molly is brought to George Washington. The general said, "henceforth you will enjoy the rank of sergeant, for your bravery." General Greene and Baron Von Steuben were there. General Lafayette was not there, but one of his officers represented him and said:

> He was very much taken, my general, with the young woman with yellow hair who carried water in her pitcher and took her husband's place in battle. He and some of us, some of his men, have put together a small trifle, which he sends to you and I now present you, Madame, will you please take off your hat?

The French officer fills the hat with coins, and that explains the title of the book.

At the end of the book there was an author's note that I read carefully because it explained what parts of the story were real history and which parts Marjory Hall had made up. I learned that the author herself wasn't entirely sure what was true.

> Considering how little is known of Molly Pitcher, the number of contradictions and differences of opinion is surprising. A few people say she never existed—but much good money has gone into the granite and bronze of monuments to honor a mere myth. Some say she was Irish, born Mary Macauley, although Macauley appears actually to have been the name of the man she married after

> her first husband's death. Most contend she
> was Mary Ludwig, of German extraction

Marjory Hall said that John Hays, the Irvines, and the generals she mentions were real. She didn't put Lafayette himself in the final scene because he was not in a painting of the scene that is in a museum at Freehold, New Jersey, and she was very doubtful that anyone gave her a hatful of gold.

> Still it is a pretty legend, if that's what it
> is, or perhaps just a fanciful tale invented
> by a biographer somewhere along the line.
> I would like to think that for her courage
> and her steadfast devotion to her country,
> even in the unusual circumstances of having
> been under fire, she was rewarded in this
> picturesque manner by the dashing French
> general, whose lively fancy would surely have
> been taken by the picture of a young woman
> staunchly fighting for her country.
>   Let's put it this way: If she wasn't really
> so honored, it would have been a nice touch.

Marjory Hall had a page of acknowledgements telling where she made her research trips and naming the people who helped her. And at the very end of the book was a three-page bibliography. Her book was much closer to real history than *Molly Pitcher: Young Patriot*. But even after all her research there were things she wasn't sure about— for instance Molly Pitcher's real name.

I wasn't expecting much from the picture books, but in some ways they were more helpful than the novels. The pictures were made up, but no one had a camera at the

Battle of Monmouth, so all the pictures—even the one that Margery Hall had looked at in that New Jersey museum—were based on imagination. Both Jan Gleiter and Kathleen Thompson's *Molly Pitcher* and Anne Rockwell's *They Called Her Molly Pitcher* showed Molly as Irish with red hair.

Molly Pitcher said the heroine's name was Mary Hays and her friends called her Molly. Her husband's name was John. She had married him when she was fifteen while she was working as a servant. At the Battle of Monmouth she heard men calling, "Water! Water!" and so she grabbed a pitcher and filled it at a spring. In this book, John Hays is not wounded but collapses from exhaustion in the heat. All the other members of his gun crew keep on working. But the loss of one man is bad enough, so Molly picks up John's ramrod and takes over, giving the order to load as she packs the gunpowder into the cannon. At the end there is nothing at all about any reward or meeting with general officers.

They Called Her Molly Pitcher, repeated the name Mary Hays but said her husband's name was William, not John. Husband William was wounded by a musket ball. Other men continued working the cannon; and, as in the other picture book, Mary takes over with the ramrod. George Washington gives her the rank of sergeant, and the book ends saying that Mary Hays never called herself Molly Pitcher even though the soldiers did. "As long as she lived, she asked everyone to call her Sergeant Molly."

I took all four books downstairs to check them out even though I knew books from the children's section wouldn't look very impressive on my preliminary bibliography list.

"I found a couple of things down here for you, Peggy," Ms. Guelphstein said. She handed me a book called

Women in Battle. "Look at chapter ten," she said. "And I xeroxed an entry from a reference book called *Notable American Women.* You'll like this one. It's short, but it has a bibliography."

"Fantastic!" I said and gave her a hug. If I hadn't already decided to be a private investigator like Greatgramps when I grew up, I thought I would want to be a librarian. Like Greatgramps, Ms. Guelphstein seemed able to find the answer to every possible question.

I took my treasures home and spread them out on the kitchen table. Then I opened my social studies notebook to take notes.

"Not that way, Peggy." Greatgramps came in and sat down next to me. "If you make your notes that way, you'll never be able to find what you want when you start writing. More important, you won't be able to make connections as you go."

"So what do I do?"

"Let me show you my system for solving mysteries and maybe we can adapt it for your search." Greatgramps went up to his bedroom and brought back a long box. It was about the size of a shoebox but speckled black and white like a composition notebook. Inside were packs of index cards held together with rubber bands.

Greatgramps took out a pack, removed the rubber band, shuffled the deck, and fanned the cards on the table. "The secret is color coding," he said. He quickly pulled out all of the blue cards and showed them to me. "Blue is for witnesses," he said. "Contact info on the front and my notes on their credibility on the back. For you these would be bibliography cards. Let's see," he said and picked up *They Called Her Molly Pitcher.* "The credibility of this one is pretty low. If I were making out the card, I'd write 'kid's picture book.'"

"Does that mean I can't use it?"

"You can use it if you want to. If you need a list of titles by next week, you may have to. But a few months from now when you have a stack of blue cards and notes from a lot of them repeat the same thing, you may decide to put this one on the bottom of the pile." He examined his stack of blue cards. "For instance in this case," he said, "I had seven people who could identify the man driving the white truck. Five of them were average citizens. One was a six-year-old kid, and the seventh was a deaf mute who used sign language and printed notes on a pad to communicate. Well, I didn't need seven witnesses; Five was plenty. So two of these witness cards didn't get used."

"I guess all of the books I found in the children's section would get classed with the six year old kid, but they gave me ideas for some things I could follow up."

"And that's why there are yellow cards," said Greatgramps grinning and flashing one from his stack. "Yellow cards are for 'bright ideas.' What ideas did you get out of these books?"

I looked through the notes I'd made on lined paper in the spiral notebook. I already had enough to get confused. I looked up at Greatgramps who was twiddling his thumbs and looking at the ceiling as if to say, "look at how I'm not saying I told you so."

I finally found the note I wanted. "I have a list of generals that the books say knew about Molly Pitcher and were there when George Washington made her sergeant and who praised her in front of witnesses. The Stevenson book said there were thousands of soldiers watching so that the whole army knew about her. I could check in histories about those generals and see if there are any more details or maybe footnotes to primary sources. Here are quotations I copied."

I read from my notebook. "General Knox says 'All America will be proud of you, not only today and tomorrow but forever.' General Greene says, 'You are a heroine, Sergeant Molly. Your name will go down in history.'"

"Those words are testimony," said Greatgramps. "They go on white cards with a code connecting it with a blue card plus the page number you took it from. Of course you can't trust them any more than you trust the source, but if you can get the facts corroborated, then you have something important. So on a yellow card you write: check biographies of Generals Knox and Greene. A stack of yellow cards is like a 'to do' list when you go to the library."

"Most of the cards will be white," I said.

"Sure. After all, facts are fundamental; but the blue and yellow cards will keep your research moving. Just as I had witnesses to interview, you will have books to locate and read. And just as my yellow cards reminded me what questions I wanted to ask witnesses, yours will remind you what you want to find when you read. When witnesses got talking they'd want to tell me all sorts of things that were fascinating but not relevant. I couldn't afford to waste the time; I was billing clients by the hour."

I figured I couldn't afford to waste time either.

"What's that book?" Greatgramps asked pointing at Laffin's. "That one looks like it came from the adult shelves."

"It did. There's a lot of neat stuff. Listen to this part about George Washington and Molly Pitcher:

At one time she wanted help to take a weighty and boiling camp kettle from the fire and asked a passing soldier to lend a hand. The man obeyed so promptly and without the usual mock objections that she said, 'What's *your* name?'

'George Washington,' the soldier replied, and acknowledged the curtsey she gave him.

"Sounds unlikely to me," said Greatgramps, "unless Molly Pitcher was feebleminded. Everyone connected with the army would know what the commander-in-chief looked like. Besides, he wouldn't wander around the camp wearing rags like the enlisteds did. He'd always be in his general's uniform."

"But Laffin says right here, 'We have the story from Washington's own pen.' I wish Laffin had put footnotes in his book to make it easier to find the quotation from George Washington."

"I'd think the absence of footnotes was a reason to doubt the credibility of the book. But maybe there is a source for the story that you'll run across eventually."

"Here's a part I want to put on a yellow card," I said finding another place in the book. "Everything I've read so far is saying Pitcher was not her real name, and that she was called Pitcher because she used a pitcher to carry water to soldiers. Now that just seems wrong to me."

"You've got a hunch," Greatgramps smiled.

"Yeah," I smiled back. A hunch. I took a yellow card from the spare pack in Greatgramps's box and wrote, "How did women carry water during the Revolution? Didn't they use pails and poles across their shoulders?"

"Good question," said Greatgramps when I handed it to him. "But a pail of water would be pretty heavy. The old saying goes, 'A pint's a pound the world around.' A gallon is eight pounds. A big pail might hold a couple of gallons or more, and you say women would be carrying two."

"That isn't so much." I said. "Anyway, let me find the part in Laffin that got me thinking. He says, 'About this time Mary became known as Molly Pitcher, presumably because of the water jug she carried among the sick and wounded.' Now how big was the biggest pitcher you ever saw? Maybe two quarts? That's four pounds. A little kid could carry that much. But right after he says this stuff about the pitcher, he writes, 'She is said to have been so strong that she threw an injured man over her shoulder and carried him from a battlefield. This is no doubt true, for there is the witnessed incident of her finding a Private Dilwyn left for dead among a pile of corpses. She carried him to safety and with great patience and the most devoted nursing restored him to health.'"

I put down the paper and imitated Greatgramps laying down the law, "It seems to me that a woman who can carry dead weight over one shoulder isn't about to tiptoe over a battlefield carrying water in a bitsy pitcher."

Greatgramps laughed. "You'll want a yellow card about this Private Dilwyn, too. 'A witnessed incident,' the man says. Yes, it is too bad he didn't give you the footnote."

"This article gives sources," I said and showed him the xerox from *Notable American Women*. The entry says the woman known as Molly Pitcher was Mary Ludwig Hays McCauley who seems to be the same person the other books are talking about. The bibliography includes her obituary notice."

I knew about obituaries. When my grandmother died, there were several paragraphs in her hometown newspaper that gave all the facts of her life—when she was born, her parents, her husband, her children and grandchildren, and all the charitable organizations she volunteered for. If I could get Molly Pitcher's obituary from her hometown newspaper, written by someone who knew her and describing her action at Monmouth, I would have a genuine primary source. Maybe I'd also have the correct version of her name.

The obituary had appeared in a newspaper dated January 26, 1832. I wondered how anyone had been able to find a copy of a newspaper that old. I made a yellow card to ask Ms. Guelphstein.

- six -
Moll Pitcher of Lynn

A few days later I received a letter from Mrs. Spinner. It wasn't really a letter because it was written
on thick paper folded together into a kind of package and sealed with red wax. My name and address with
the zip code was written on the outside sheet in old-fash-
ioned handwriting. Except for the zip code and the modern
stamps, it could have came through a time machine.

> *My dear Miss Peggy,*
>   *I am pleased to inform you that my search*
> *for Pitcher military records uncovered the*
> *names of 23 men named Pitcher who served*
> *in the Continental Army listed in one book*
> *and 28 men listed in another. This is, no*
> *doubt, an embarrassment of riches for you*
> *since searching for the names of wives of so*
> *many men would be time consuming even for*
> *an experienced genealogist. Colonial military*
> *records do not list dependents.*

Nevertheless, all is not lost, for in sorting through my papers, I have come upon materials relating to one Moll Pitcher who was a resident of Lynn, Massachusetts at the time of the Revolution. Her husband may not have served in the Continental Army—his name was not in my books—but at that time all men who were not elderly or disabled served in the militia. Mrs. Pitcher herself was quite famous. I would be happy to share my files with you should you wish to pursue this line of investigation.

I am at home to visitors at teatime on Wednesdays and Fridays and shall be pleased to receive you should you care to pay a call.
Very truly yours,
(Mrs.) Alice Spinner

I got out my collection of research notes. I'd bought a plastic storage box for index cards at the dollar store. Greatgramps said they didn't make the cardboard kind he used any more. I'd found colored index cards and dividers at the supermarket, and I had a pad of yellow stickies to mark individual cards so I could find them again. I took out some pink ones.

Greatgramps used pink cards for suspects. I now had too many people to keep track of in my head. I would copy down all the Pitchers from Mrs. Spinner's books. If any of the names came up again, I would be prepared.

My prime suspect so far was Mary Ludwig Hays McCauley, if that was the right spelling. I decided to make a bunch of cards for her using all the different names and spellings. By using Greatgramps's system of coding to witnesses, I would eventually discover who was reliable and which name to use when I wrote the report.

I was certainly curious about Moll Pitcher of Lynn, but the name alone wasn't enough. I would have to find out why she was famous before I made her a suspect.

On Friday afternoon I went to visit Mrs. Spinner by myself. Greatgramps said it would be all right for me to dress normally since I had already been introduced, so I wore my usual jeans and sweatshirt. Mrs. Spinner was still eccentric, wearing colonial clothing and spinning rabbit fur, but this time she was clearly pleased to see me.

"Look Fluffy, here comes Miss Peggy," she sang out as I crossed the bridge. "You'll have to go back in your hutch now so Miss Peggy and I can discuss historical research."

She led the way into her parlor, which was less purely colonial than it had been at my first visit. Books were scattered about, most of them in modern bindings, and a red plastic file tub rested on the floor in front of the fireplace. A heap of manila folders covered the tea table.

"Let's look at these before we have tea," she said. "I am so excited to have found them again. I had quite forgotten I had them."

We sat in the straight-backed chairs as she told me about Moll Pitcher of Lynn.

"You see, my dear, I had once thought of writing something about Mrs. Pitcher. History, of course," she added looking at me over the top of her spectacles. "I first learned about her from a long poem by John Greenleaf Whittier. You do know Whittier, don't you?"

"Uh, huh," I said. "I mean, yes, ma'am. He wrote the poem about Barbara Fritchie."

Mrs. Spinner beamed. "It is so nice to meet a young person who knows the classics. 'The clustered spires of Frederick stand/ Green-walled the hills of Maryland,'" she recited.

"'Shoot, if you must this old gray head,/But spare your country's flag, she said.'" I added, showing off.

"Yes, yes," Mrs. Spinner beamed at me and leaned forward in her chair. "Now 'Moll Pitcher: A Poem' isn't nearly so well known. It is a much earlier work, published in 1832, but listen to this verse." She adjusted her glasses and began to read:

> A wasted, gray and meager hag,
> In features evil as her lot.
> She had the crooked nose of a witch
> And a crooked back and chin
> And in her gait she had a hitch
> And in her hand she carried a switch
> To aid her work of sin.

I gulped. No matter how famous she was, this Moll Pitcher would never qualify as a great American hero.

Mrs. Spinner noticed my expression and quickly responded. "She wasn't really like that, Miss Peggy. I just wanted to show you how famous she was." She put down the book of Whittier's poems and consulted a piece of notepaper. "One Joseph Stevens Jones wrote a novel about her called *Mollie Pitcher, the Fortune Teller of Lynn: a Tale* in 1843 and produced it as a play a few years later. Another novel about her was published in 1895. But to get the true facts, this is the book you go to."

She handed me a book from a stack on the floor. I could tell that it was very old. The binding flaked off a little on my hands when I touched it. I turned to the title page and read *History of Lynn, Essex County Massachusetts: including Lynnfield, Saugus, Swampscot, and Nahant* by Alonzo Lewis and James R. Newhall.

"Alonzo Lewis actually knew Mrs. Pitcher," Mrs. Spinner said, "and everything else written about her goes back to this book."

"So why was she famous, if she didn't do 'work of sin'?" I asked.

"She was a psychic," said Mrs. Spinner, "a fortune teller as they used to say, and a very good one. Ship owners consulted her because she could foretell storms. She had hundreds of clients from all walks of life, and tradition had it that General John Glover of Marblehead took her to Cambridge to see General Washington. She told him that the patriots would win the war."

"Well, I can see that would make her popular," I smiled, "but this doesn't sound like the woman I'm writing about."

Mrs. Spinner's face fell. "Oh dear," she said. "I seem to have gotten carried away. Of course you must keep to the topic of your assignment." She sighed. "Pity. There is much more documentary evidence about Moll Pitcher of Lynn than about the other Molly Pitchers."

My ears pricked up. "Did you say Molly Pitchers? Is there more than one?"

"Oh yes," said Mrs. Spinner. "At least two—one Molly at a cannon at the Battle of Monmouth and another Molly at the Battle of Fort Washington."

Before I left Mrs. Spinner's house I copied the 23 names of soldiers named Pitcher from *Revolutionary War Records*. I also made a note on a yellow card to look for a woman named Molly at the Battle of Fort Washington.

seven

Mary Hays

I was feeling rather pleased with myself when I handed in my preliminary bibliography. Mr. Pettibone wanted three secondary sources and I had six. I also listed my two primary sources: *Revolutionary War Records* and the 1832 obituary notice. I knew Mr. Pettibone would cross those out, but he would know I had material to do a first class research paper.

When we discussed the assignment in class, I realized I was the only one who had gone to the library. Everyone else had used computers to go on the web. I'm the only kid in my class whose family doesn't have a computer, and I hadn't thought of using the computer in the library except for the book catalog.

Mr. Pettibone said that skill in searching web sites would be essential for anyone doing research in the twenty-first century which was coming up fast. Living with Greatgramps, who never even watches television except for old movies, I was firmly stuck in the twentieth. Mr. Pettibone gave us some instructions about search engines and gave us some web addresses. Everyone but me seemed to know about these already. Mr. Pettibone said the best one was something called Google. That afternoon, I went back to the library and asked Ms. Guelphstein for help.

I typed in Molly Pitcher for a web search and got a gazillion hits. I tried Mary Hays and got a gazillion. Ms. Guelphstein said that the most popular web sites were listed first although that didn't necessarily mean they were the best.

"Just play with it for a while," she suggested. "Sometimes you get lucky."

I tried keying in some combinations like "Molly Pitcher and Battle of Monmouth" but still got the gazillions. I printed out some pages that were among the couple of dozen at the top of the list but they all seemed to say the same thing. Or rather, they didn't say the same thing. Like the books I found, they agreed that Mary Hays was Molly Pitcher, but they disagreed as to whether her maiden name was Ludwig, exactly when she was born, what her husband's name was, and how her second husband spelled his name. They all mentioned the Battle of Monmouth and the woman at the cannon, but none of them had a contemporary source to link Mary Hays with that woman. I wanted proof. What I need, I said to myself, is a smoking gun—a smoking cannon.

Then I tried the genealogical approach and looked for some of the 23 Pitcher soldiers whose names were listed in *Revolutionary War Records*. I found a genealogy page, keyed in "Molly Pitcher," and hit pay dirt. At least I thought I had, but the person posting seemed more confused than I was. "My Great Great Grandmother was Molly Pitcher She was a friend of Pocahantus [sic] and our relatives were originaly [sic] from Penn. and migrated to Ok. and Mo." Later she explained, "My 3 back greats grandmothers maiden name was Ludwig I believe she is also the Molly Pitcher of P.A.I am new into this side of family geneology [sic] just starting just now working on it."

Pocahontas had been dead for at least a century before Molly Pitcher, whoever she was, was born, but I traced this thread to see if the woman who posted ever got any useful information. Maybe I could at least find out for sure if Mary Hays's maiden name had been Ludwig.

Someone tried to help by forwarding the message from the Pitcher list to the list for the McCauley Family under the heading "Mary Hayes or Hays Heis McCualy." There was an exasperated response: "I am so sorry I don't know how I got on the McCualy family???? I am working on the Moyer Family."

Ms. Guelphstein came by to see how I was doing. I was pretty exasperated myself. "I got titles of some more secondary sources," I told her, "but I don't think they are going to help. All these pages seem to copy from each other, and I can't tell where the story started." I told her about Moll Pitcher of Lynn and how Mrs. Spinner had identified the book that all the later writers used. "I wish I could find a book like that," I said. "A book by someone who actually knew Mary Hays."

"Internet research has its limitations," Ms. Guelphstein said, "especially when you are new to it. Why don't you try this: Arrange your bibliography notes according to publication date. See what are the oldest things you can find. Even if you don't get the very first source, you will be closer."

I pulled out the stack of blue cards from my backpack. I had been writing down all the citations whenever I found something with footnotes or a bibliography. I knew which one was the oldest.

"Here's my oldest source," I said. "I didn't think I'd be able to find it." I showed her the card for the obituary notice cited in *Notable American Women*. It said "Am. Volunteer (Carlisle), Jan. 25, 1832."

Ms. Guelphstein took the card, sat down at the computer, and began to type. She flew from one page to another so fast I couldn't keep track and eventually came to a page that linked to early American newspapers. I got so exited I was bouncing up and down. Then just when I thought we had it, a screen came up saying that to get access, I'd have to buy something called AncestryView CD-ROM. It cost a lot of money.

"I'm sorry, Peggy," Ms. Guelphstein said, "but we don't have this in our library." I must have looked as if I was about to bawl. "I'll tell you what I can do," she said. "I have librarian friends at the historical society and at the university. I can ask them if they can get to the nineteenth century Carlisle newspapers and do a search for Mary Hays and 1832 and print out the results."

"Would they do that?" I asked. "That would be a lot of work, wouldn't it? And they don't even know me."

"They don't know you, Peggy, but they know me," Ms. Guelphstein laughed. "Librarians do things for each other they wouldn't do for an ordinary library patron. We trade favors. Anyway, if you have the CD, it is really quite simple to find newspaper articles."

I hugged her so hard I nearly knocked her out of her chair. "Now, you'll have to be patient, Peggy," she said. "I am sure I can get this material for you eventually, but my contacts may not get to it right away."

"That's okay," I said. "I don't really have to have it until next term when we start writing our reports." Then I had another idea.

"If I find titles of real old books that aren't in our library could you get those for me?" I was convinced now that there was probably nothing Ms. Guelphstein couldn't find.

"Not all books," she said, "but I can get most things for you through interlibrary loan. Is there anything in particular you want?"

I shuffled through my cards, looking at the publication dates and found what I was looking for: *"Molly Pitcher": A Short History of Molly Pitcher, the Heroine of Monmouth* by John B. Landis, published in 1905. On the back of the card I had written that the book was based on interviews with people who had actually known Mary Hays.

"Could you get this?" I asked.

Ms. Guelphstein took the card and began to tap at the computer keys. She frowned. "Are you sure you copied this card correctly?" she asked. "This book does not appear to be listed at the Library of Congress."

"I copied it from a bibliography," I said.

"Well it seems to be from a small publisher. It may have been privately published for the author. Let me check library holdings." She tapped some more keys.

"The Pennsylvania State Archives have a copy," she said. "And the Historical Society Library has one. But it is classified as a rare book so it won't go out on interlibrary loan."

"What if I got Greatgramps to drive me? Could I look at it there?"

"I'm afraid not, Peggy. You have to be at least a college level student to get into those collections."

I sighed. What did they think? That just because a person was only in eighth grade they'd use highlighter in a rare book? I knew it would be no use fighting it. Kids don't have equal rights with grownups. We can't vote even for things like school board where we know a lot more about the issues than our parents do. And so it's no surprise we don't have equal rights in libraries.

"Peggy, you are doing a fantastic job of research on your project. I never expected that you would be able to find as much as you have. Don't push yourself so hard. Maybe some day you'll write a Ph.D. dissertation on Molly Pitcher, but you don't have to do that much for Mr. Pettibone—or even to win the Rattletop Award."

I tried not to look as annoyed as I felt. I just hate it when people tell me not to push myself or not to be so intense or to stop trying so hard. I like to push myself; that's just the way I am. Why should other people care—it's not like I'm telling them to work as hard as I do.

So I insincerely smiled sweetly, thanked Ms. Guelphstein very sincerely for all her help, and slammed the door behind me when I got home.

"Uh, oh," said Greatgramps from the kitchen. "Have a hard day in the salt mines?"

I dumped my backpack in the hall and marched into the kitchen where I dropped into a chair prepared for a good sulk.

"Tell me about it," Greatgramps demanded. He was stirring something on the stove.

"It's nothing," I said.

"Sure. So give me the details on this nothing."

"There's this Molly Pitcher book. It's like eyewitness evidence; at least it's close to that. It has information from people, a lot of people, who actually knew Mary Hays. They probably heard her talk all the time about the Battle of Monmouth and how George Washington made her a sergeant and all those other things that I haven't been able to get sources for. It's my smoking cannon," I said liking the sound of the phrase.

"So what's the problem?" Greatgramps said.

"I can't get to see the stupid book!" I wailed. "There are copies locked up in libraries because it is a rare book, and I won't be able to look at it until I am old!"

"How old is old?" asked Greatgramps. "Am I old enough?"

"Probably," I snorted, "but it's not your research project."

Greatgramps washed his hands at the sink and sat down at the table.

"You don't have to have the smoking cannon to make progress in an investigation. How's the timeline coming?"

The last assignment we had on our research papers before Christmas was to make a list of known facts about our hero with footnotes to different sources. It's a pass/fail assignment because Mr. Pettibone said he will only grade the final product. Still, my timeline was giving me trouble. The main fact was I was really short of provable facts about Molly Pitcher even after all my weeks of work.

"So far I have at least two versions of where she was born, a maiden name that may or may not be correct, two possible years of birth, at least four possible names for her first husband, and six or eight spellings for the name of her second husband. I have a firm date of death. And I guess I can put in her being at Valley Forge and at the Battle of Monmouth even though I don't have any primary source to confirm that."

"And the assignment isn't due until when? Late December, isn't it? I'd say you are doing very well."

- eight -
The Real Mary Hays

The timeline due date came fast, and I did have a life besides Molly Pitcher. The school band was doing a Christmas show, and I had a piccolo solo. I was taking a tap dance class on Saturday mornings that my mother signed me up for because she thought I didn't get enough exercise. And then, of course, I had classes.

English was reading books and writing book reports, which I enjoyed. It didn't even seem like real work to get class credit for reading and writing. Science was easy if sometimes smelly. The only class I had to work in to keep my straight A average was math.

I kept plugging away on Molly Pitcher, but I wasn't making much progress. I found out that census records and tax records proved that Mary Hays's first husband was named William and that they had a son who was born in 1780 according to one source or 1782 according to another.

A week before the assignment was due, an envelope arrived from Ms. Guelphstein's friend with not one but two obituary notices for Mary Hays McCauley. I read them eagerly. The first was the one from *The American Volunteer,* January 26, 1832

> Died on Sunday last, in this borough, at an advanced age, Mrs. Molly McCauley. She lived during the days of the American Revolution, shared its hardships, and witnessed many a scene of "Blood and carnage." To the sick and wounded she was an efficient aid, for which; and being the widow of an American hero, she received during the latter years of her life, an annuity from the government. For upwards of 40 years she resided in this borough; and was during that time, recognized as an honest, obliging, and industrious woman. She has left numerous relatives to regret her decease; who with many others of her acquaintance, have a hope that her reward in the world to which she has gone, will far exceed that which she receive in this.

That was all! No mention of the Battle of Monmouth and no mention of a cannon! Her husband is called an American hero, but she's just the widow! I picked up the other obituary. On January 26, 1832 *Carlisle Herald* wrote:

> Died on Sunday last, Mrs. Mary McAuley (better known by the name of Molly McAuley) aged 90 years. The history of this woman is somewhat remarkable. Her first husband's name was Hays who was a soldier in the war of the Revolution. It appears she continued with

him in the army and acted so much the part of the heroine as to attract the notice of the officers. Some estimate may be formed of the value of the service performed by her, when the fact is stated that she drew a pension from the government during the latter years of her life.

Again nothing about the battle or the cannon. Nothing about being called Molly Pitcher or even Sergeant Molly. I had a sinking feeling that I might have spent the whole term following the wrong lead and would have to start all over again with a new suspect. I had a pink card for Margaret Corbin, whom I'd identified as the Molly at Fort Washington, but I hadn't researched her at all.

When I settled down at the kitchen table two days before the timeline assignment was due, I made some firm decisions. For now, I would assume that Mary Hays was Molly Pitcher. I could put Valley Forge and the Battle of Monmouth in the timeline because even if I wasn't sure myself, I had lots of footnotes. Most of the other facts were still a tangle.

I spread out my white "facts" cards and decided to start from the beginning. That would be with Mary Ludwig.

I was awfully glad that Greatgramps had shown me how to use index cards because otherwise I would never have been able to sort things out. I had a bunch of fact cards from different sources that said that Mary Ludwig was born on October 13, 1754 but none of them gave a source for that information. One book, the oldest, said the date was October 13, 1744. The *Carlisle Herald* obituary said Mary Hays had been 90 when she died in 1832, which would mean she was born in 1742. The entry in *Notable American Women* used the 1754 birthday but had a question mark next to it. I could see a good reason for that when I considered the next recorded "fact," Mary Ludwig's date of marriage.

A Pennsylvania marriage license was recorded on July 24, 1769, for Mary Ludwick [sic] and Casper Hays. If that woman was the same as Mary Ludwig and had been born October 13, 1754, she would have been 14 years old.

Fourteen seemed awfully young to me, so I had asked Ms. Guelphstein how old girls had to be to get married in the eighteenth century. She found a book that gave statistics on ages for first marriages for women. On the frontier it was 19 and 18 in Virginia, but for Quaker and German women in the Delaware Valley it was 24, an older age than in any other part of in America. A fourteen-year-old bride would definitely have been unusually young.

I looked at my stack of "first husband" cards. Some books said Mr. Hays's first name was William, and I was sure that was right. Some books said John Casper (or Caspar) Hays. Most said just plain John Hays, and none of them said Casper Hays.

Before I was sure about William Hays being Mary's first husband, I had asked Mrs. Spinner to find out if a John Hays from Carlisle had served in artillery in the Continental army. She found records for one John Hayes and one John Hays who had been in the Continental Army but no John Casper (or Caspar) and no plain Casper (or Caspar) Hays either. And neither of the John soldiers had come from Carlisle where Mary's husband was supposed to be from. So where did Mary's John Hays from Carlisle come in? The name rang a bell, and I shuffled through some other cards. There it was: William and Mary Hays had a son named John.

I put my elbows on the table and my fists in my hair while I tried to get the story straight. "Once upon a time," I muttered, "there was a girl named Mary Ludwig who, at the age of fourteen years and nine months, married her own son."

"Stop trying so hard, Peg," Greatgramps said.

I took a deep breath and tried to relax. "That's the way, Peg," Greatgramps said approvingly. "Don't sweat the small stuff. Why don't you just pretend to be a normal kid, and do this assignment? After Christmas vacation you can dig into the research again and tie up the loose ends."

I went back to listing "facts." October 13, 1754. That was supposed to be Mary Ludwig's birthday. Maybe I could go with the one source that gave the year as 1744, which fit better with the other facts —but Mary Ludwig was not the woman who had married William Hays. Whatever the year, October 13 was Mary Ludwig's birthday, not the birthday of Mrs. William Hays.

I was getting myself in a tangle again. I held my nose as Greatgramps would say and put down my first timeline "facts" even though I knew they were wrong. The dates were in most of the books and would satisfy Mr. Pettibone:

- October 13, 1744(?) born Mary Ludwig near Trenton, New Jersey (forget about the books that said Philadelphia)

- July 24, 1769 married William Hays, a barber (forget about Casper and forget about everyone named John)

- 1777 follows husband William Hays who had enlisted in the Pennsylvania Artillery (I was sure this was true—if it hadn't been Mary Hays wouldn't have got a pension— and I knew where to look for enlistment records.)

- 1777–1778 winters with husband at Valley Forge (I was pretty sure this was true. Where else would she be? I footnoted the Historic Valley Forge web site because it sounded official.)

- June 28, 1778 loads and fires a weapon at the Battle of Monmouth (I didn't have proof yet that she had done either, but plenty of secondary sources said so, so I went for both.)

- 1786 William Hays dies. Mary remarried sometime before 1793 to John McCalla (many variations of spelling because both John and Mary were probably illiterate; Mary signed her name with an x.)

- October 3, 1806 received two hundred acres of land "for services rendered in the Revolutionary War by her late husband William Hays of Proctor's 4th Artillery, Continental Line" (document in National Archives Record Ser Group 93)

- February 21, 1822 granted a pension by the state of Pennsylvania "for services rendered in the Revolutionary War." (proved by published *Laws of Pennsylvania*)

- January 22, 1832 dies in Carlisle, Pennsylvania (proved by two obituary announcements)

nine

More Primary Sources

Greatgramps and I do our Christmas shopping at a Salvation Army store in Philadelphia. A little money goes a long way there. If you have a good eye for quality, you can find amazing bargains.

Greatgramps drove us to the store in his sticker-covered car on the Saturday before Christmas. Mom always works weekends during the holiday season for the extra pay. She doesn't like to shop at the Salvation Army anyway. She says that's for poor people, and she uses her discount to do her shopping at Wal-Mart.

We split up inside the store; we always keep what we buy secret so on Christmas morning all the packages are a surprise. Then we drove home and wrapped our gifts right away. That's a tradition to prevent snooping. After that we baked Christmas cookies and while they were still warm wrapped them as gifts for friends and neighbors.

I took a box of cookies to Mrs. Spinner and another one to Ms. Guelphstein at the library the day before Christmas. I didn't expect them to have presents for me, but they did. Mrs. Spinner's was in a large flat red box decorated with a sprig of real holly. Ms. Guelphstein gave me a white envelope that looked like it contained an ordinary Christmas card, but she said that I was to put it under the tree and not open it before Christmas.

In the weeks before Christmas, I was usually asleep before Mom got home from work, but I waited up with Greatgramps on Christmas Eve. The two of us had trimmed the tree, and when Mom got home we had a little party. I had cocoa and cookies; Mom and Greatgramps had brandy. When I was small and believed in Santa Claus, Mom used to say that Santa got tired of cookies and milk and what he really liked to find when he came to fill up stockings was a glass of brandy. So I used to leave brandy by the fireplace. When I grew older I realized that brandy was Greatgramps's idea of a treat.

Mom and I got to talking about Molly Pitcher. Even though my research project was a big deal to me, Mom hadn't been home enough for me to talk to her about it.

"Molly Pitcher! What a wonderful subject! I always loved her. I remember a book I read when I was a girl. Something about George Washington and gold coins."

"Is this the one, Mom?" I still had *Hatful of Gold* on loan from the library.

"Oh, my," Mom said looking at the picture of a pretty blond girl in dainty shoes on the cover, "such a romantic story this one was."

Christmas was the first day in a long time that Mom didn't have to get up early to go to work, so she slept late. Greatgramps and I had an early breakfast and set the table in the dining room. When Mom came downstairs in her robe and fuzzy slippers, he served what he called "brunch," and then we went into the living room to open our presents.

Mom hadn't had time to wrap very well, but Greatgramps and I enjoyed our surprises. Mom bought Greatgramps an electric grill so he could make his summertime specials in the winter, and I got a pair of running shoes that all the popular kids in school were wearing this year. I knew they must have really stretched Mom's budget, but I couldn't help squealing with pleasure when I put them on. Even a weird kid likes to be in style.

Mom gasped when she saw her gift from Greatgramps— a real gold bracelet with tiny diamonds. The people at the Salvation Army had priced it as costume jewelry, but Greatgramps could tell by the weight that it was the real thing. I'd done pretty well as Santa Claus too—I'd found a cashmere sweater in Mom's favorite shade of blue. The size six sweater was brand new with the tag from a fancy store still attached.

I was especially pleased with myself for what I'd found for Greatgramps. He likes to do jigsaw puzzles, the really hard kind with thousands of pieces. They cost a lot if you buy them new, but it's important to buy an unopened box. If just one piece is missing it spoils the whole project. This year I found a bunch of complicated puzzles still sealed in plastic. They must have been too hard for the person who got them as gifts.

"Open that one," Mom said pointing to the red box Mrs. Spinner had given me. "That one will be a surprise for everyone."

The box contained a brown paper accordion file tied with red tape and a note in Mrs. Spinner's elaborate penmanship:

> *Dear Miss Peggy,*
> *For many years I collected images of Molly Pitcher from divers sources as they came to*

hand thinking I might one day arrange them in an album. As I have put off doing so for so long, I have concluded that I never shall. And so I pass my collection on to you, hoping that it pleases you and that it might amuse you some rainy day to arrange the images in a book.

I opened the paper file and a multitude of Molly Pitchers spilled onto the carpet. Most were photographs or xerox copies, but others were colorful images on glossy paper clipped from magazines or advertising flyers. A tiny cellophane bag held two postage stamps one identified with the year 1928 and another as 1947. There was a newspaper clipping about what was called a "Liberty ship" named SS *Molly Pitcher* that was launched in 1943 and torpedoed the same year. At the bottom of the pile I found a bumper sticker of Molly and her cannon and handed it to Greatgramps with a grin.

"Ah, just what I have been looking for," he said. "This will make a nice balance to 'Defend Your Right to Arm Bears.'"

The biggest box under the tree was my gift from Greatgramps. When I was little, he used to buy me a huge pile of presents, but now that I'm older I get one special gift instead of a lot of little things. I always save my gift from Greatgramps for last.

I attacked the box, ripping off the paper. That was another family tradition. Inside was another wrapped box. Oh, ho! One of those. I ripped some more, scattering the paper around the room while Mom and Greatgramps laughed. Finally I came to a small flat package wrapped in plain brown paper.

Inside, covered with a plastic wrapper, was a thin book in a worn dark green cloth cover. On the spine in gold were the words "Molly Pitcher." It was a copy of the Landis, *Short History*. I sighed with pleasure, bent my head to read and did not look up until I had finished all 58 pages.

"Earth to Peggy," Mom said. "Are you still with us?"

I blinked and stared at Greatgramps. "But how did you...? You didn't steal it from the Historical Society, did you?"

"Of course not," Greatgramps harrumphed. "I'm an officer of the court."

"But Ms. Guelphstein said this is a rare book."

"It is. But rare books are for sale. There were not many copies printed, but not many people want them these days. It's not as if it were a new Alicia Spinnaker novel." Greatgramps chuckled at his private joke. "I have a friend who helps me do online shopping. I bought this on the web from www.abebooks.com. I was lucky, of course. Rare books are not always listed for sale when you want them."

"This is amazing," I said stroking the book. "It has a lot of mistakes in it because the people quoted were real old when it was written in 1905, but they remember meeting Mary Hays and what she looked like. Like here's something from her grandson," I said finding the page. "'In her old age he heard her speak a great deal about her army experiences, and he often heard from her own lips the story of the battle of Monmouth, and of her participation in it, giving the facts as they have been already detailed.' I don't trust him, though, because just before this he was saying that his father was born in a tent on the battlefield at Monmouth. Can't you just see that?" I said. "Molly does all her heroics at the cannon and then goes into labor right on the spot." Mom and Greatgramps laughed.

"And there's this old lady…" I turned to the next page, "Miss Harriet Foulke said that Mrs. Hays 'was so well known as 'the Molly Pitcher' of Monmouth, that no effort seems to have been made to perpetuate a fact which all seemed to recognize.'"

"Is that supposed to explain why it's not in writing anywhere until long after her death?" Greatgramps asked.

I shrugged. "This book is no smoking cannon," I said, "but it is still pretty amazing. There are some neat pictures in it too. Look at this one: it's supposed to be a pitcher Mary Hays owned." I handed the book over to my Mom.

"Looks like Chinese import ware," she said. "It's quite small, isn't it? Is this the one she carried on the battlefield?"

"I guess people would think so what with it being labeled as Molly Pitcher's pitcher," I said, "but I don't believe it. Who'd carry a fragile little china pitcher on a battlefield? Anyway the book admits that some people believe she used a cannoniers' bucket—the artillery needed water to swab out the cannon. The engraving of Molly Pitcher at the front of the book shows a wooden bucket."

"There is something familiar about this picture," Mom said, still studying the Molly Pitcher pitcher. "Peggy, let me see that *Hatful of Gold* book again."

I handed it to her and Mom paged through it.

"Here we are!" she said triumphantly. "Molly is about to head off toward the battlefield and it occurs to her that the men would want water on such a hot day, so she goes to a farmhouse and asks the woman there for something to carry it in. Listen to this:

"Do you," Molly asked hesitantly, "have an extra bucket or an old pitcher of some kind? The men will need water in this dreadful heat."

"My husband is a cannoneer, poor unhappy man," the woman said indifferently. "They have buckets, you know, for wetting the sponges to swab out the cannon."

"Then Molly explains how her husband is also serving in artillery, and the farmwoman points her toward the dresser: 'There is a pitcher there. See it? It's gray or black, with some heathenish buildings with strange curly roofs on it. '"

Mom looked up with a grin. "That's the same pitcher all right. And in *Hatful of Gold* Molly has the same doubts we do: 'Molly saw the pitcher. It was smaller than she had hoped, only eight or nine inches in height, but it was fat and of course better than nothing.'"

We all laughed.

"I can see you'll be filling out a lot of index cards from this book," Greatgramps said. "Guess I did a good Santa Claus bit this year."

"Oh yes, Greatgramps," I said springing up to hug him. "This is just the most amazing gift." I went to hug Mom too. "And the shoes are cosmic," I added. "This has been a terrific Christmas."

"There's still something left," Mom said. "What's that envelope?"

"Oh, I almost forgot," I said reaching for it. "This is from Ms. Guelphstein at the library."

The envelope did contain a Christmas card, but it also held a small xeroxed newspaper clipping neatly identified on the back as (New York) *National Advocate*, March 7, 1822. The Christmas card included a note.

Dear Peggy,

One of my librarian friends ran across this while she was looking for something else. I thought this item was special enough to be considered a Christmas gift. Lots of love and Happy New Year,
Gillian Guelphstein

March 7, 1822—that was just a few weeks after the Pennsylvania Legislature voted to give Mary Hays her pension. I read the brief notice: "Molly Macauly [sic], who received a pension from the State of Pennsylvania for service rendered during the Revolutionary War, was well-known to the general officers as a brave and patriotic woman. She was called Sgt. McCauly [sic] and was wounded at some battle, supposed to be the Brandywine, where her sex was discovered."

I gasped. Here was a primary source confirming the story about her being called Sergeant, but no cannon and an entirely different battle. "Her sex was discovered"—that meant she had been disguised as a man! So maybe when they called her "sergeant" it wasn't just a cute nickname for a brave woman. And wounded at Brandywine—that was the biggest battle in the whole war!

I read further and gasped again, "It was not an unusual circumstance to find women in the ranks disguised as men, such was their ardor for independence." The article named another woman I'd never heard of: Elizabeth Canning. I'd have to give her a pink card. Then I read a sentence that seemed to have been written just for me. "It would be interesting to collect anecdotes of the services rendered by women during the revolutionary war."

- ten -
A Wider Perspective

I would have spent the rest of Christmas day with my stack of index cards, but Mom and Greatgramps wouldn't allow it. Then I guess they got their heads together because Mom was afraid I was going to retreat into my books and index cards and wouldn't get any fresh air or exercise until school started again. Anyway, after dinner when I was helping Greatgramps with the dishes, he asked if I'd like to visit the crime scene.

"The weather forecast says clear weather will hold until the weekend," he said. "We can start out early tomorrow and be at Carlisle by 9:30 or 10:00, have a look around and then hit Valley Forge on the way back. The old sticker-mobile can get some time on the highway, and you can give your new shoes a workout."

"Sounds great," I said.

Neither of us had counted on the weather being quite so cold. Greatgramps's car has a super motor, but the heating doesn't work too well. The sun was just rising when we started out the next morning dressed in our warmest clothing. Mom had already left for work. The day after Christmas is a busy shopping day with everyone out exchanging gifts or buying themselves things they'd hoped they'd receive but hadn't.

Greatgramps packed a picnic hamper so we wouldn't have to stop for meals. We had a big thermos of coffee for him and one of hot chocolate for me. We each had a cup right away while the car was warming up.

Greatgramps loves to drive. Once we hit the open road on the Pennsylvania turnpike, he started singing. He began with the Marine Corps hymn like he always does and then sang a couple of Christmas carols, a love song that was popular seventy-five years ago, and the toreador aria from the opera *Carmen*.

"Any requests," he asked as he ran out of inspiration.

"How about a story," I said. "Were any of our family in the Revolution?"

"Ah, you'd like to hear some family history would you? Well everyone who lived around here back then was in the Revolution. You couldn't get out of it." He paused to think a moment. "My grandfather mostly told me Civil War stories, but let me see what I can remember him telling me about the really early days." Greatgramps sucked his moustache as he searched his memory.

"First off," he said, "we came over on the Mayflower."

"Greatgramps!" I said. "There wasn't anyone named McAllister on the Mayflower."

"Now who said I was telling the story according to the direct male line of descent?" he said. "This is an indirect line going back on my great-great-great-etcetera-grandmother's side." He took his eyes from the road for an instant to see if I was paying attention. I was. I'd never heard this story before.

"Our first ancestor in America was named John Alden and he married this gal named Priscilla." Now I was almost certain Greatgramps was pulling my leg, but before I could interrupt he rushed ahead. "They had a bunch of kids and the youngest was named Patrick Alden."

Now I was positive this was a gag, but I went along with it. "So your first name is a hand me down from an early American ancestor and not from one of those immigrant McAllisters," I said.

"Exactly," Greatgramps said looking pleased with himself. "Well it seems that young Paddy Alden got bored living on that rock in Plymouth, so one day he packed up his bags and moved to Boston."

Uh, huh, I thought, knowing that Boston wouldn't have been any improvement on the "rock" back in the early seventeenth century.

"And when he gets into town," Greatgramps continued, "he stops at an ale house to grab some lunch and hears some feller talking about plans for a wild ride that night out in the country."

"And that feller was named Paul Revere, I suppose," I said.

"Right you are, Peggy, the very same."

"And I suppose young Paddy McAllister, I mean young Paddy Alden, volunteered to go along."

"He sure did. And they had a swell time. And the next day there were a couple of battles..."

"Lexington and Concord," I said.

"Right you are, again," Greatgramps said. "And Paul Revere was so impressed with my ancestor that when they got back to Boston he introduced him to this girl he knew named Betsy Ross."

By this time I was laughing and Greatgramps could no longer keep a straight face.

"Now your grandfather didn't really tell you that story, did he?" I demanded.

"Not quite that way," Greatgramps admitted, "but his Civil War stories were almost as inventive. His military records show that he didn't enlist until the fall of 1864, and he lied about his age to get in then. But when he was old, like me now," he chuckled "ol' Grandpa used to go on for hours about his experiences at Gettysburg."

"And the moral of all this is that you can't trust family history unless it's backed up with documents."

"Something like that," Greatgramps said.

"And these monuments we're going to look at are all based on tales told by folks like your ol' Grandpa."

"I didn't exactly say that," said Greatgramps, "but isn't that what you've been telling me? Like that man who said Molly Pitcher gave birth to his father in a tent at the Battle of Monmouth?"

"I wish some of the people John Landis quoted in his book had mentioned something about Brandywine," I said wistfully. "Newspaper stories can be as bad as family histories in getting facts mixed up. So now I don't believe the story about Mary Hays being at a cannon at Monmouth, but I wouldn't want to say I was sure she was a soldier at Brandywine either."

"Why don't you take a turn providing some entertainment, Peggy? Tell me about the Battle of Brandywine."

So I told Greatgramps what I had learned about the fighting in the fall of 1776 that ended when Washington took his army into winter quarters. I thought Greatgramps must have learned all this stuff when he was in school, but he always listens to me explain things. I think he realizes I learn things best when I can talk about them.

"In July 1777, the part of the British army commanded by General Howe left New York City by sea. General Washington was up there watching and knew when they left. But he didn't know where they were going. He thought maybe they were going north to try to cut New England off from the other states. But it turned out they were going south to try to capture Philadelphia where the Continental Congress was. Once he was sure about that, Washington marched his army south as fast as he could and met the British army at the Battle of Brandywine. That's September 11, 1777. He had more soldiers all at one time than he would ever have again, and this was the biggest battle of the war. A thousand American soldiers were killed, and the American army had to retreat. Then there was the Battle of Germantown in October, and the Americans had to retreat again. That sounds bad, but it really wasn't because the soldiers didn't run away. They did what they called 'an orderly retreat' and George Washington still had an army.

"While this was going on, there were two forts guarding the mouth of the Delaware to keep the British ships from sailing up and getting at Philadelphia that way. Eventually, the Americans at the forts had to give up. Washington decided there wasn't any way he could stop the British from taking Philadelphia now, and with winter coming on he took his army to Valley Forge hoping they could do better in the spring."

"Where was Mrs. Hays and the other women like her while all this was going on?" Greatgramps asked.

"They were marching with the army," I said. "The history books don't talk about them much."

"I suppose not," Greatgramps said. "Even though women were there. Did you know there were women serving where I was in the South Pacific during World War II? Not just nurses either. They lived in the mud and got shot at, but when you read about World War II, you never hear about them."

I hadn't known that. Maybe when I finished writing about Molly Pitcher, I would try to learn about the World War II women.

When we got to Carlisle, Greatgramps took us straight to the Molly Pitcher grave. He always studies the maps before he goes anywhere, and we never get lost. People stared at us as we drove through the streets. Greatgramps said it was because of his license tag that says "WW2VET" as if that would get more attention than a car covered with stickers. We parked and walked around the Molly Pitcher gravesite.

I had seen pictures of the Molly Pitcher memorial—the monument and the statue and the flag by a cannon. A patriotic organization had bought the cannon in 1905, but I was sure the tourists who came to look would believe it was the authentic Molly Pitcher cannon. I liked the statue; seeing it full size I could imagine Molly Pitcher as a real person. She definitely looked like a hero. The stone monument had mistakes on it. The biggest, I thought, was saying the woman buried there was Molly Pitcher. But I already knew how mixed up the people of Carlisle were when they decided to honor Mary Hays. As Mrs. Spinner might say, you had to give them credit for trying to honor their history at a time when it was much harder to do research.

We didn't stay long in Carlisle, because Greatgramps said there was a lot more to see at Valley Forge and it would be getting dark early.

We made good time driving back east. Greatgramps has a conspicuous car, so you'd think he'd worry about being stopped for speeding. But he has these electronic gadgets to warn him when to slow down, and if these don't work he plays his role as old World War II vet when the police make him pull over and gets off with a warning.

Valley Forge wasn't a battle, but more than twice as many soldiers as died at Brandywine died there in the winter of 1777-1778. We went first to the Visitors Center where it felt good to warm up. There was a wonderful exhibit with equipment used by the women camp followers as well as weapons and things that belonged to soldiers and officers. We watched a film, got a map and went out to look around. Coming out of the Visitors Center, it felt even colder outside.

On weekends, when the weather is good, visitors can watch a reenactment of what life was like for soldiers at Valley Forge. Another demonstration shows how Von Steuben trained the soldiers so that they performed like European armies when they left the camp in the spring. I was sorry that we had missed the reenactments. Greatgramps said he'd bring me back again in the summer when there were more activities, but I knew it wouldn't seem as real as it did for us standing out in the December cold.

We looked at the drafty wooden buildings and tried to imagine what it must have been like for the men and women who lived in them. We stayed at Valley Forge until the sun began to set and Greatgramps drove fast to try to beat rush hour around Philadelphia. Neither of us felt like talking much on the way home, and between the cold and all the walking, I fell asleep.

- eleven -

A Box of Pictures

Once the after-Christmas shopping rush subsided, Mom got to take some time off. She took me out in the old Honda she has to drive to work. We went to the museum in Philadelphia one day and to the movies at the mall on another, which we don't do very often because it's so expensive; but Mom had saved up some extra dollars so we could splurge. We stopped to eat in fast food restaurants. Greatgramps disapproves of them, so getting burgers, soda, and fries was really special for me. The best thing was that Mom and I had time to talk and to catch up with each other.

I tried not to talk too much about Molly Pitcher. Mom is proud of my being smart, but she worries about me not being "well rounded." Of course, I had to tell her all about Mrs. Spinner and Mr. Pettibone, but I also made a point of talking about band practice and gym class and silly things kids did in study hall.

Mom told stories about her friends at work. Even though they worked hard, they had time to talk and laugh together. Mom knows all about her co-workers' families and the problems they have with their health. It's like mom has a crowd she hangs out with the way the popular kids do at school. I found myself wondering if the women following the army with Mary Hays joked and laughed together when they were doing laundry or cooking or going out to gather firewood.

On the last day of vacation, it snowed. I took the broom and swept the porch and the steps while the snow was still falling to keep it from piling up. When it stopped, Greatgramps wanted to go out with the shovel, and we got into an argument because I didn't want him to. Greatgramps is in good shape for his age, but he is looking pretty hard at ninety. Fortunately, one of the neighbors got a snowplow for Christmas. While Greatgramps and I were arguing, he came by and plowed out our driveway. Greatgramps gave him a box of cookies and offered him some money, but he wouldn't take it.

"So if I can't go out to play in the snow, what can I do?" Greatgramps said. I laughed.

"Why don't we go through Mrs. Spinner's picture box and look for evidence," I said. "If there are any more bumper stickers, you can have them."

"Unless you find a book that says Molly Pitcher drove a car to the Battle of Monmouth, I suppose you can safely give those away," Greatgramps said.

I brought the box to the kitchen table.

"What I want to do is pull out the oldest ones," I said. "Maybe there are some in here that were done by people who actually knew Molly Pitcher."

"I can work from the other end," Greatgramps said. "It's easier to pull out the pictures that are recent like my bumper sticker." He began to pick out calendars and advertising flyers, a book of matches, a restaurant menu, a brochure for a hotel in Red Bank, New Jersey near the site of the Battle of Monmouth called the Molly Pitcher Inn.

"Now this might be worth some money," he said picking up a cellophane envelope. "This is what we call an overprint with Molly Pitcher stamped on it that goes back to 1928." He put the envelope to one side and continued his dig.

"Here's something to put with the stamp," I said, fishing a stiff rectangular card from the pile.

"Nice," said Greatgramps. "It's a prestamped postcard issued September 8, 1978. I used to collect stamps when I was a boy. Maybe I'll take it up again."

I found two road maps that I passed over to Greatgramps. One showed a stretch of US route 11 ending at the Pennsylvania-Maryland state line known as Molly Pitcher Highway and another identifying a rest stop on the New Jersey Turnpike named for Molly Pitcher. "This goes with bumper stickers," I said. "Mrs. Spinner certainly was thorough in collecting stuff."

"There's a fair amount of World War II material in here," said Greatgramps. His share of the loot was growing faster than mine. "Old, but not old enough for your purposes, Peggy," he said. "And of course there is lots here from the bicentennial years back in the 'seventies."

We sorted in silence for a while with each of us making our own subcategories. I could see why Mrs. Spinner thought her Molly Pitcher collection would make a good scrapbook although I didn't think I would ever want to spend the time it would take pasting and making labels any more than she did.

"These belong in their own category," I said, moving one of my stacks to the side of the table. "These are from

Molly Pitcher memorials—the one we just saw at Carlisle and the big one at Monmouth."

"These things from New York State should probably go with them," Greatgramps said. He showed me a photograph of a memorial stone from Fort Tryon Park in New York City and another at West Point. He also had a copy of a watercolor painting that was in the West Point Museum. "These sure look like Molly Pitcher," I said, "but look at the name on them: Margaret Corbin."

"That's a new one," Greatgramps said. "Who's she?"

"She's another suspect. I haven't gotten around to researching her yet, but I have some other pictures here that are supposed to be her." I showed him a program for a bicentennial memorial service for Margaret Cochran Corbin on 12 November 1976 at Letterkenny Army Depot in Chambersburg, Pennsylvania. The program cover had a sketch based on the West Point watercolor combined with a more familiar drawing of Molly Pitcher at Monmouth. "And look at this announcement from the Order of Molly Pitcher. It's a special award for women married to artillerymen but the picture they use is of Margaret Corbin."

"I've heard of that award," said Greatgramps. "The women who have it are very proud of it, and they have a fancy medal they wear."

"Here's another bunch of stuff from something called the Corbin Society that seems to be for students at the military academies. I think these should go in their own folder until I learn more about Margaret Corbin."

"What is the oldest picture you've found?" Greatgramps asked examining a photocopy he'd just picked up. "Whatever it is, I bet this one is older."

I looked at what I had. "The oldest is 1848 done by Nathaniel Currier of Currier and Ives although he hadn't started working with Ives yet."

"Well I got you beat," Greatgramps chortled. "Look at this. Without a doubt the oldest and probably the ugliest drawing ever done of Molly Pitcher." He pushed the photocopy across the table. The picture was a crude woodcut that showed a huge smirking women with a fancy hat decorated with flags standing on an island with ships in the water all around. She was astride a cannon with her skirt pulled up firing the cannon from between her legs. The picture was titled "The Taking of Miss Mud Island." and marked "printed in London in 1777."

"Mud Island was where one of the forts guarding the Delaware River was," I said. "But even if this is supposed to be a real woman, it can't be Molly Pitcher because the Battle of Monmouth wasn't fought until June, 1778."

"Why not? You've got a woman and a cannon and a source dated during the American Revolution."

I wrinkled my nose. "I think this Mud Island lady is even worse than the witch from Massachusetts."

"Are you after the truth about Molly Pitcher or just looking for evidence that she was the hero you'd like her to be?"

"I want the truth, but I think it's jumping to conclusions to think just any woman with a cannon is supposed to be Molly Pitcher"

"Who else would it be?"

"Joan of Arc, maybe," I said. I really didn't want to have Molly Pitcher turn out to be this ugly Miss Mud Island.

Greatgramps guffawed. "This Mud Island lady is no saint," he said. "But you're right; there were other women in history who fired artillery pieces." He looked thoughtful for a moment and then got up and went to his bookshelf in the living room.

Greatgramps doesn't own many books—he says that's what libraries are for. But he has a few, and one of them is a big picture book, a history of western art. I thought he was going to find some paintings of Joan of Arc, but what he brought back to show me was very different.

"Goya," Greatgramps said. "Early nineteenth century." The picture was titled *Que valor!* and showed a woman in what looked like a long white nightgown walking over the bodies of dead or wounded men and, yes, firing a cannon.

"She's real," said Greatgramps, his eyes sparkling. "In fact, she's famous—at least she was famous in the nineteenth century."

I read the description under the picture. The woman was Agostina of Saragossa. The drawing had been "romanticized," the book said. Actually the woman Agostina had worn the uniform of a captain of artillery in the Spanish army and had been in command during a battle during the Napoleonic Wars.

"Pretty cool," I said, "but my assignment is to write about an American hero."

I opened my box of index cards.

"Get a brainstorm?" Greatgramps asked.

"Maybe," I said. "While I've been taking notes I kept trying to find the real name of the woman at the cannon and wasn't paying too much attention to what the sources called her. I think the 1848 print I just found could be the oldest reference calling her Molly Pitcher. I thought I'd try sorting the notes from primary sources by date the way I was doing with the pictures."

"Molly Pitcher, the Heroine of Monmouth"
by Nathaniel Currier 1848 (Library of Congress)

"The Taking of Miss Mud Island"
Broadside by an anonymous artist 1777 (Library of Congress)

Que valor !

Engraving of Agostina of Saragossa by Francisco de Goya
from a collection of his prints called *Disasters of the War*
first published in 1863

On June 28, 1812, exactly 34 years to the day after the Battle of Monmouth, the woman known as "The Maid of Saragossa" was observed by hundreds of witnesses in an act of valor during a French attack on the Spanish town of Saragossa. The French broke through the outer wall of the town and killed all the men at artillery positions. Agostina climbed to the ramparts, took a lighted match from the hand of a dead soldier, and fired the artillery piece he had failed to set off before he was killed. Then she reloaded the cannon and fired again. Inspired by her example, other civilians resisted the invaders at the guns and in street fighting. The French withdrew. After the battle, the duke of Saragossa gave Agostina a number of medals, authorized her to take the name of the town she defended as her surname, and granted her the pay and pension of an artillery captain. When she died, after a long life as a European celebrity, Agostina was buried with military honors.

Molly Pitcher Monument, Carlisle, Pennsylvania

twelve

A Box of Index Cards

I had a little trouble finding the oldest piece of evidence because I hadn't been sure where to file it. I found it quoted in one of my books. It was a diary entry dated July 3, 1778, just a few days after the Battle of Monmouth. The diary belonged to Albigence Waldo, a doctor from Connecticut. He was an Army surgeon who had treated the wounded at Monmouth. His diary was published in 1840. He wrote:

> One of the camp women I must give a little praise to. Her gallant, whom she attended in battle, being shot down, she immediately took up his gun and cartridges and like a Spartan heroine fought with astonishing bravery, discharging the piece with as much regularity as any soldier present. This, a wounded officer whom I dressed, told me he did see himself, she being in his platoon, and assured me that I might depend on its truth.

This was proof, just one step from an eyewitness, that a woman had fired at the enemy at the Battle of Monmouth. The trouble was, she hadn't fired a cannon. She "took up" her husband's weapon—you don't lift a cannon—and her ammunition was "cartridges." So she would have been a heroic woman at the Battle of Monmouth, but not Molly Pitcher.

I didn't have any trouble finding the second oldest source, which was the prize of my collection. The reminiscences of Private Joseph Plumb Martin were published in 1830, but there were modern editions so I was able to read a copy in the library. Private Martin had been at the Battle of Monmouth and wrote:

> One little incident happened during the heat of the cannonade, which I was an eyewitness to, and which I think would be unpardonable not to mention. A woman whose husband belonged to the artillery and who was then attached to a piece in the engagement, attended with her husband at the piece the whole time. While in the act of reaching a cartridge and having one of her feet as far before the other as she could step, a cannon shot from the enemy passed directly between her legs without doing any other damage than carrying away all the lower part of her petticoat. Looking at it with apparent unconcern, she observed that it was lucky it didn't pass a little higher, for in that case it might have carried away something else, and continued her occupation.

This was a funny story, and I'd have thought someone made it up as a joke, except that Private Martin said he was an eyewitness. All the story did, really, was to show there was a woman working at a cannon. She was passing ammunition, not loading or firing, and her husband remained in good health. Maybe later on, her husband had been wounded and the woman took up another role, but that would just be a guess. As in Waldo's account, the woman Martin describes has no name. If she was with her husband "the whole time," she could not have been carrying water during the battle as Molly Pitcher was supposed to have done.

A section in my file box had a bunch of fact cards in rubber bands from two really neat sources that Ms. Guelphstein got for me through interlibrary loan. The items were just a few pages long, so the libraries had sent her xerox copies.

The first xerox Ms. Guelphstein got for me was a little booklet called *A Molly Pitcher Chronology*. The *Chronology* booklet was only sixteen pages long, but it was very well organized and packed with good information including footnotes to primary sources. There were quotations from more people who had known Mary Hays that would go in the section of my note file with the testimony from the book Greatgramps had given me. Reading them was interesting, but all of these quotations came from long after Mary Hays had died and had a marker on her grave stating with authority that Mary Hays definitely was Molly Pitcher.

I shuffled through the notes I had made from the *Chronology* and found what I was looking for: a quotation from a pension application. Rebecca Clendenen applied for a widow's pension on May 12, 1840 saying that her husband,

John Clendenen "often mentioned to this respondent the toils and fatigues which he underwent and related particularly that he was at the Battle of Monmouth, and suffered greatly with the heat and thirst, that a woman who was called by the troops Captain Molly was busily engaged in carrying canteens of water to the famished soldiers." No cannon, no Molly Pitcher, but the widow was a living link to the battle.

The second xerox Ms. Guelphstein got for me was an article called "Goodbye, Molly Pitcher" by D. W. Thompson that was published in a magazine called *Cumberland County History* in 1989. That wasn't so long ago, so you'd think it would be easy to understand, but it wasn't. The organization was hard to follow. There were some facts in it that I copied onto cards, but there were others in it I didn't really need to know—like records that in April 1811 the County Commissioners paid fifteen dollars to "Molly McCalley for washing and scrubbing the court house."

I thought about how Mr. Thompson had read all those primary sources and wondered if I'd ever want to do that. I imagined him sitting in a library reading tax records day after day and every once in a while saying, "Yippee! Here's a mention of Mary McCauly!" and writing it down.

The reason "Goodbye, Molly Pitcher" was so confusing was explained in an "Editor's Head Note." It seems that Mr. Thompson died before the article was finished and a second writer, Merri Lou Schaumann, added some genealogical research. Then the editor of the magazine had to try to put it all together and add footnotes. The xerox copy Ms. Guelphstein gave me didn't have the name of the editor, but I thought that person deserved a lot of credit.

The best notes I got out of "Goodbye, Molly Pitcher" were from very old rare books, the kind I'd never be able to borrow and were much too long to xerox. The oldest was by George Washington Peale Curtis, the same man who had painted the first picture of a woman at the Battle of Monmouth. Thompson said that Custis was "the chief begetter of the story of the cannoneer-heroine at Monmouth."

Custis was Martha Washington's grandson from her first marriage. Martha was a widow when she married George. Custis's father was killed at Yorktown and his grandmother raised him. The article doesn't say what happened to his mother. Anyway, he must have known George Washington pretty well although he was away at school a lot of the time and was only eighteen when Washington died.

Custis liked to write and in the late 1820s began to publish stories based on his memories of his stepgrand-father. In 1840 all of them were reprinted in something called the *National Intelligencer*. I went back to look again at my note on Mrs. Clendenen's petition. It was dated 1840. Maybe she had read Custis's Captain Molly story and it had colored her memory of what her husband had told her. I made a note of that possibility and went back to my notes on Custis.

After Custis died, his George Washington stories were published as a book called *Recollections and Private Memories of Washington* in 1859. It must have been popular because the next year a second edition came out.

I copied quotations from Mr. Thompson's article. The Custis stories are the very first report of the heroic actions of a woman cannoneer at the Battle of Monmouth although they were written by a man who hadn't been born at the time and who wrote about them sixty years after the battle. Of course everyone who read the book assumed that George Washington had given Custis the details.

This is what Custis wrote in a chapter called "The Battle of Monmouth":

> At one of the guns of Proctor's battery, six men had been killed or wounded. It was deemed an unlucky gun and murmurs arose that it should be drawn back and abandoned. At this juncture, while Captain Molly was serving some water for the refreshment of the men, her husband received a shot in the head, and fell lifeless under the wheels of the piece. The heroine threw down the pail of water, and crying to her dead consort, "lie there my darling while I revenge ye" grasped the ramrod the lifeless hand of the poor fellow had just relinquished, sent home the charge, and called to the matrosses to prime and fire. It was done. Then entering the sponge into the smoking muzzle of the cannon, the heroine performed to admiration the duties of the most expert artilleryman, while loud shouts from the soldiers rang along the line; the doomed gun was no longer deemed unlucky, and the fire of the battery became more vivid than ever. The amazonian fair one kept to her post till night closed the action, when she was introduced to General Greene, who, complimenting her upon her courage and conduct, the next morning presented her to the Commander-in-Chief. Washington

received her graciously, gave her a piece of gold and assured her that her services should not be forgotten.

This remarkable and intrepid woman survived the Revolution, never for an instant laying aside the appellation she has so nobly won, and levying contributions upon both civil and military, whenever she recounted the tale of the doomed gun, and the famed Captain Molly at the Battle of Monmouth.

This is definitely the Molly Pitcher story, but Custis doesn't call her Molly Pitcher. I noticed that he said she was carrying water in a pail not a pitcher. And Custis is clear that her honorary rank was captain, not sergeant.

Custis wrote about the same woman again in a chapter called "Headquarters":

Among the great variety of persons and characters that were to be found from time to time at and about Headquarters, was the famed Captain Molly. After her heroic achievements at the Battle of Monmouth the heroine was always received with a cordial welcome at Headquarters, where she was employed in the duties of the household. She always wore an artilleryman's coat, with the cocked hat and feather, the distinguishing costume of Proctor's artillery. One day the Chief accosted this remarkable woman while she was engaged in washing some clothes, pleasantly observing: "Well, Captain Molly, are you not most tired of this quiet way of life, and longing to be once more on the field of battle?" "Troth, your Excellency," replied the heroine, "and ye may say that; for I care not how soon I have another slap at them red coats, bad luck to them." "But what is to become of your petticoats in such an event, Captain Molly?" "Oh, long life to your excellency, and never de ye mind them at all, at all," continued this intrepid female. "Sure, and it is only in the artillery your Excellency knows that I would sarve, and divil a fear but smoke of the cannon will hide my petticoats."

A teacher once told me that the way you could tell the difference between novels and history was that novels had conversations in them and that in history books all the quotations came from letters or diaries. I thought Custis was probably like the people who write scripts for docudramas on TV. He rearranged things and made up conversations to make a better story. Even so, this was the first time anyone had published something about Captain Molly.

Captain Molly. Again, not Molly Pitcher. But this was definitely the Molly Pitcher story.

Next, Thompson's article talked about Benjamin Lossing's *Pictorial Field Book of the Revolution*, the book with the sketch copied from Curtis's painting of the Battle of Monmouth. Thompson says the book was very popular and he says the long footnote Lossing had for the Battle of Monmouth came from what Custis had told him:

It was during this part of the action that
Molly, the wife of a cannonier, is said to have
displayed great courage and presence of
mind. We have already noticed her bravery in
firing the last gun at Fort Clinton. She was a
sturdy young camp-follower, only twenty-two
years old, and, in devotion to her husband, she
illustrated the character of her countrywomen
of the Emerald Isle. In the action in question,
while her husband was managing one of
the field-pieces, she constantly brought him
water from a spring near by. A shot from the
enemy killed him at his post; and the officer
in command, having no one competent to fill
his place, ordered the piece to be withdrawn.
Molly saw her husband fall as she came from
the spring, and also heard the order. She
dropped her bucket, seized the rammer, and
vowed that she would fill the place of her
husband at the gun and avenge his death. She
performed the duty with a skill and courage
which attracted the attention of all who saw
her. On the following morning, covered with
dirt and blood, General Greene presented her
to Washington, who, admiring her bravery,
conferred upon her the commission of
sergeant. By his recommendation, her name
was placed on the list of half-pay officers for
life. She left the army soon after the Battle of
Monmouth, as we have before observed, died
near Fort Montgomery, among the Hudson
Highlands. She usually went by the name
of "Captain Molly." He described her as a

stout, red-haired, freckled-faced young Irish woman, with a handsome piercing eye. The French officers, charmed by the story of her bravery, made her many presents. She would sometimes pass along the French lines with her cocked hat, and get it almost filled with crowns.

So here's where the hatful of gold started and the commission of sergeant too. But where did Captain Molly come from? Was she the same as Molly Pitcher?

I took out the Nathaniel Currier print and looked at again. The title was "Molly Pitcher, the Heroine of Monmouth." Currier made the print in 1848. That was seventy years after the battle. I was sure I didn't have any Molly Pitcher sources older than that. The 1832 obituary notices didn't say anything about Molly Pitcher or about Monmouth. Mrs. Clendenen's 1840 pension claim said "Captain Molly." Neither of the eyewitnesses describing a woman at the Battle of Monmouth used the name. So where did Currier get it?

The only explanation I could think of was that Currier had heard the name of Moll Pitcher of Lynn and either got confused because she was a famous eighteenth century woman or he just decided he liked the sound of the name. He certainly didn't invent the name thinking about the way the heroine of Monmouth carried water to the troops. He drew her with a bucket, not a pitcher. Unless I eventually found something earlier, I'd have to give Currier credit for naming Molly Pitcher of Monmouth.

- thirteen -
In Search of Captain Molly

I'd been putting off looking for evidence about Margaret Corbin. When I finally went to the library to find out about her, I was surprised how easy it was. You'd think with Mary Hays being identified by everyone as the real Molly Pitcher and practically no one mentioning Margaret Corbin that it would be much harder to find evidence about her. But I found plenty of stuff in just one day.

There were no books in the children's section, and they wouldn't have footnotes anyway. I went straight to *Notable American Women* where Ms. Guelphstein had found the first good evidence about Mary Hays. The article said, "Only the barest facts are known about her," but at least what was known was clear.

I collected fact cards and bibliography cards from the *Notable American Women* article and from other reference books on the shelf. I went online to see if everyone agreed on the facts or if there were contradictions the way there were with Mary Hays. There were a few, and I wrote them down.

After just a couple of hours, I got out my social studies notebook and made a time line the way I had for Mary Hays.

- November 12, 1751 born Margaret Cochran in Franklin County, Pennsylvania

- 1756 father killed by Indians; mother captured and never returned. Margaret and brother go to live with mother's brother

- about 1772 marries John Corbin from Virginia

- 1776 John Corbin enlists in the Continental army as a private in Proctor's artillery. Margaret becomes a camp follower

- November 16, 1776 Battle of Fort Washington. John Corbin is killed. Margaret takes up his position at artillery piece and is wounded. Taken prisoner by the British and after her release returns to Pennsylvania with permanent disability: loss of use of one arm

- June 29, 1779 Pennsylvania Supreme Council allows her thirty dollars relief because of her "heroism and helpless situation"

- July 6, 1779 Continental Congress grants her a pension

- 1780–1783 enrolled in Invalid Regiment, West Point, New York

Only for the end of her life was there disagreement. Official records using the name Margaret Corbin end in 1783 when the war ended and the Invalid Regiment was disbanded. Some sources said she returned to Pennsylvania, died in Westmoreland County on January 16, 1800 and was buried in the graveyard at Congruity, Pennsylvania. Other sources identified her with a woman known only as "Captain Molly" who died about 1800 in the village of Highland Falls, New York. I would have to sort this out later.

We had an assignment due at the end of January to turn in a "progress report" on our research projects. Mr. Pettibone wanted to be sure no one tried to do all the work at the last minute. By the end of February we had to have finished all our research and turn in an outline. The progress report was supposed to be one page long and say what we had accomplished so far and what we still had to do.

I really tried, but I couldn't fit all my progress into one page. Just the list of sources I'd read filled up more than that. Finally, I squeezed everything into three pages by using a really small font when I typed it up on the school computer. Mr. Pettibone gave me a "pass" but told me to use the "standard font" the next time I turned in an assignment. And he put red lines across the last two pages meaning he hadn't read them.

Up until now, I had sort of blown off Mr. Pettibone as being a jerk. That's what Greatgramps says to do when someone gets on your nerves but you have to put up with it. Greatgramps likes to tell "butter bars lieutenant" stories about World War II when some young officer without any experience would give stupid orders to the enlisted marines who really knew what they were doing. Once the "looey" had read a map wrong and ordered the platoon into a swamp where they discovered enemy soldiers were all around. They had to stay real quiet in the mud with all the slimy things around their legs and insects biting them until it got dark and they could sneak away. One of the marines was so mad when they got back to base that he punched the lieutenant in the face and knocked him down. "They court-martialed the guy," Greatgramps said, "even though he was absolutely right, and we never saw him again."

The moral was supposed to be that sometimes you just have to "bite your tongue" or "grin and bear it" or "suck it up." That's what I'd been doing all year with Mr. Pettibone, but when he turned back my progress report with nothing but complaining about the typeface and crossing out the part where I explained the problems I still had, I lost it. By the time I got home that afternoon I was bawling.

"I was stupid to think he would help me," I gulped out once Greatgramps got me to settle down. "Probably he couldn't even if he wanted to. He doesn't know anything about Molly Pitcher. It's just that I've worked so hard and collected so much great stuff, and now I don't know what to do with it."

Greatgramps made sympathetic noises and brought me hot chocolate and cookies, but when I started to talk about how my list of suspects kept growing with Captain Mollys proliferating and names of women who had fought as regular soldiers turning up and still not having any proof for a woman firing a cannon at the Battle of Monmouth, his eyes started to glaze over. Not that I hadn't babbled about these things before, but I'd been excited about finding facts and suspects and hadn't been asking for help.

"Gee, Peg," he said. "You've gotten out of my depth here."

"That's the trouble," I wailed. "I think I've gotten out of everybody's depth. I've got more information about Molly Pitcher than anyone else ever collected, but nobody understands what I'm talking about when I say I need to find out about Elizabeth Canning or get the real name of 'Dirty Kate'"

"Mrs. Spinner would understand," Greatgramps said. "Why don't I phone her and see if she is receiving callers this afternoon?" I nodded and blew my nose. I was in no condition to make a phone call myself.

I heard Greatgramps at the phone in the hall. His murmured half of the conversation was punctuated by laughter. He was talking for a long time. When he came back he was whistling and stroking his moustache.

"Mrs. Spinner is a most delightful lady," he said, giving me the feeling that she had been flirting with him over the phone. "She said to come by whenever you please, that 'the latch string is out.'"

"Oh, Greatgramps," I said and hugged him hard, "you are always able to solve my problems."

"Since 1962," Greatgramps said quoting from his business card.

I washed my face, packed up the evidence file of Molly Pitcher photocopies and my box of index cards in my backpack and headed off through the park and over the creek to Mrs. Spinner's house.

The pine tree outside Mrs. Spinner's back door was still decorated as it had been at Christmas time with strings of cranberries and popcorn and little wooden bowls with seeds and lumps of fat for the birds. I approved. Birds didn't know about Christmas and would appreciate edible decorations all winter. Inside Mrs. Spinner had a roaring fire in the hearth. Her collection of Christmas cards remained on the mantel including the one Greatgramps and I had wrapped up with our cookies. Mrs. Spinner wore a long, dark red dress under her red checked apron with a red and green plaid shawl around her shoulders. If she'd put a sprig of holly in her hair, she'd look like Mrs. Santa Claus—or Mary Christmas as Greatgramps liked to call Santa's wife.

Mrs. Spinner smiled at my pile of research materials as she invited me to take a seat by the fire. "As I had hoped, you are not the usual schoolchild writing up an assignment from what you find in the encyclopedia."

"My whole class is doing research papers this year," I said. "Encyclopedias are just a start to help us find other sources."

"For you, perhaps, but I doubt whether many of your classmates have accumulated this much source material." She indicated the heap I had unloaded from my backpack and stacked on her floor. "I think you have the makings of an Inkling," she said.

"What's that?"

"Are you acquainted with the writings of C. S. Lewis and Tolkein?" she asked.

"Sure," I said. "I love their books. Lewis did the Narnia stories and Tolkien wrote *The Hobbit* and *The Lord of the Rings* books."

"Well when they were writing," Mrs. Spinner said, "Lewis and Tolkien and some other creative gentlemen formed a writer's support group they called the Inklings. They read each other's work and discussed it before it was published."

"That's just what I need," I said. "I've learned so much, but not having anyone to talk to who understands the history makes me wonder if what I think I know makes any sense. I need to talk to someone who'll tell me I'm not crazy."

"Exactly," Mrs. Spinner said. "A passion for eighteenth century history is not so common in Lindwood as it once was, and I have had few people with whom to converse about such topics since my husband passed on half a century ago. Talking to myself has become quite tedious, so I welcome a visit from a serious scholar."

I blushed. I was certainly serious—too serious to hear Mom and Greatgramps talk—but "scholar" meant someone like a college professor, and I was just an eighth grader.

"So let us be Inklings," Mrs. Spinner said. As she spoke, she poured kernels of corn into a wire basket and shook it over the flames. When the kernels had popped, she emptied the basket into a huge crockery bowl, topped it with a lump of butter from a small pewter dish, handed me a wooden bowl and took another for herself. We served ourselves buttery popcorn, added salt from two small bowls with tiny spoons, and talked as we nibbled.

"Your dear greatgrandfather tells me you have made great progress in your research," Mrs. Spinner said. "Have you found anyone as interesting as Moll Pitcher of Lynn?"

"I just finished making notes on Margaret Corbin," I said. "One source says she is the same person as 'Dirty Kate' of Highland Falls, but I'm not sure. Why would anyone call someone named Margaret 'Kate'?"

"That would be Benjamin Lossing's *Pictorial Field Book of the Revolution*, wouldn't it," Mrs. Spinner said. The dear man did marvelous work, terribly impressive the way he collected interviews from all over the early Republic from such remote places. But he did get stories confused."

"So you think 'Dirty Kate' was someone different from Margaret Corbin? What about the woman at Fort Clinton? Could that be the same as Fort Niagara?"

We went on like this for some time and understood each other perfectly. But to follow our conversation you would need to read more of my note cards, at least you would need to read the paragraph in Lossing's book where he records the testimony of two elderly people he interviewed in New York State. Lossing asked them about the Monmouth heroine George Washington Custis had described.

> Mr. Garrison remembered the famous Irish woman called Captain Molly, the wife of a cannonier, who worked a field-piece at the Battle of Monmouth, on the death of her husband. She generally dressed in the petticoats of her sex with an artilleryman's coat over. She was in Fort Clinton with her husband, when it was attacked. When the Americans retreated from the fort, as the enemy scaled the rampart, her husband dropped his match and fled. Molly caught it up, touched off the piece and then scampered off. It was the last gun fired by the Americans in the fort. Mrs. Rose (just mentioned) remembers her as "Dirty Kate," living between Fort Montgomery and Buttermilk Falls, at the close of the war, where she died a horrible death from the effects of a syphilitic disease. I shall have occasion to refer to this bold camp-follower for her bravery on the field of Monmouth, nearly nine months afterward, when reviewing the events of the battle.

"If Margaret Corbin was the same person as 'Dirty Kate' or just the same person who was known as 'Captain Molly' in the neighborhood of Buttermilk Falls," I said, "she couldn't possibly have been at the Battle of Monmouth."

"Certainly, she could never have been serving at artillery," Mrs. Spinner said. "Poor dear, with her shattered arm, she couldn't even carry water any longer."

"And with her husband dead, why would she try to follow the army? Do you think Mr. Lossing may be the one who's confused? He lived closer to the time than we do and was one of the first to write down the story, but some of what he says just doesn't seem right."

"He was closer to the time but far from an eye-witness. The people he interviewed knew an old army woman, and there was certainly more than one sick bad-tempered female living in the area in the wake of war. Lossing tried to make sense of the stories he heard and make them into one coherent narrative. Can you imagine, my dear, trying to research the Molly Pitcher history without library catalogs or Xerox machines, or even ball point pens and index cards to keep notes? All Mr. Lossing had to go on was the memories of elderly people or, even worse, people like Mr. Custis who repeated stories he remembered hearing from elderly people. Lossing did exceptionally well for his time. Yes, indeed, we must certainly give him credit. But we may surely conclude that in certain details he was confused. Oh, dear me, yes, he was confused!"

I decided to eliminate Dirty Kate as a suspect instead of trying to fit her into the person of Captain Molly.

"Anything else that is puzzling you, Miss Peggy?" Mrs. Spinner asked.

"Yes," I said. "Do you know when the British released the prisoners of war they captured at Fort Washington? I know they took Margaret Corbin prisoner along with the male soldiers, but I can't find when they let them out."

"They didn't hold the wounded long," Mrs. Spinner said. "With her arm injured as it was, the British would scarcely have been concerned about her rejoining the American forces as a combatant. I would imagine Mrs. Corbin was released with the others who were sent across the Hudson to Fort Lee. The Pennsylvania wounded were evacuated by wagon and taken to Philadelphia. It must have been a terribly bumpy ride and cold too so late in the year." I thought about that for a while watching Mrs. Spinner going back in time in her imagination.

There would be no footnotes to describe how it felt to be in pain from wounds and freezing cold being bounced along over rutty roads on the trip from Fort Lee in New Jersey to Philadelphia in the fall of 1776. I knew Mary Hays had been illiterate; probably Margaret Corbin was too. Even if she knew how to write, soldiers' wives weren't the sort who carried around quill pens and inkbottles to keep diaries or write letters. I shook myself out of my daydreaming. I was writing a history report and had to stick to the facts.

"Do you know of any mention of the name Molly Pitcher before this Currier print was published?" I rummaged in my file and passed the drawing to her.

"This was 1848, wasn't it?" I nodded. "As far as I know this is the first. Of course, someone else might one day locate something earlier, but no one has after more than a century and a half of looking. I believe it is safe to say this is the first."

"What about in a book? I have Captain Molly mentioned starting in 1840 but no Molly Pitcher."

"I know of no mention of Molly Pitcher in any document, book, or engraving prior to 1848," Mrs. Spinner said decisively.

I grinned. "Okay, then I'm going to say in my paper what you just did, that there might be a mention of Molly

Pitcher before 1848, but if there is no one has found it. And then…" I thought about how I'd frame my argument. "If Mr. Currier thought up the name Molly Pitcher and gave it to a woman firing a cannon at the Battle of Monmouth, then that is who Molly Pitcher 'really' is—the artillery heroine of Monmouth. And if that is who she is, then Molly Pitcher is a myth because there is absolutely no evidence that any woman loaded or fired a cannon. Women carried water and worked around the guns at Monmouth, but none of that counts as Molly Pitcher. There has to be a cannon and a husband at least wounded if not dead."

"That is a plausible argument, Miss Peggy," Mrs. Spinner said, "but will following that reasoning not prevent you from completing your research paper? If you prove that your subject never existed, she can scarcely be described as a great American hero."

"I thought about that," I said, "so here's what I thought I'd do. Molly Pitcher isn't real. But Mary Hays is real and Margaret Corbin is real. Maybe Elizabeth Channing and 'Dirty Kate' and some women soldiers whose names I wrote down on pink cards are real. I can argue that because everyone has been so distracted looking for the 'real' Molly Pitcher, they have ignored a whole bunch of real heroes. I have Mary Hays being wounded at Brandywine and Margaret Corbin being wounded at Fort Washington. If I can get footnotes for just one or two more, I think I can write a prize-winning paper."

"That is quite ingenious, Miss Peggy," Mrs. Spinner said. "I for one would be immensely interested in reading such a work."

I left Mrs. Spinner's house with a warm glow inside, fired up to finish my research and begin writing the prize-winning Rattletop paper.

- fourteen -
A Homeless Veteran

G reatgramps always comes home in a bad mood when he's been to see his doctor at the Veterans Administration hospital. He says it takes forever to get an appointment, and that once he's there he has to sit around and wait for hours. He says he thinks his blood pressure would be normal if he didn't have to go to the VA for his checkups.

"When we signed up after Pearl Harbor," Greatgramps roared at me, as if it was my fault, "the government promised us that if we served for 20 years we'd get lifetime health care for us and our dependents. And now that I'm old and really need it what do they do? Say they've changed their minds and I can use Medicare like the civilians. That costs $60 a month, only pays part of the bill, and doesn't pay anything until I've shelled out $100 toward the costs."

I didn't say anything. When Greatgramps gets in one of these moods, it's best to just let him blow off steam until he calms down.

"I'm getting as bad as my father and grandfather," Greatgramps muttered. "My Grandpa marched on Washington with the Civil War veterans in Coxey's army and my Dad went marching with the World War I vets in 1932. Neither of them got squat."

"At least you're not homeless," I said, forgetting I was going to keep my mouth shut.

"What's that supposed to mean? That the Vietnam vets have it worse than I do?"

"That the Revolutionary War vets had it worse, at least that the one I'm studying did."

"You told me Mary Hays collected her pension same as I collect mine. And they didn't have health care costs in those days. You gave the doctor a chicken when he came round to make house calls, and the pills he dished out didn't cost more than caviar. She wasn't homeless either— you showed me the picture of the house she lived in. Looked as good as what we've got."

"I'm thinking about the other suspect. Margaret Corbin."

"So, what happened to her?"

"She was wounded at the Battle of Fort Washington, like I told you. Total disability, lost the use of her arm. She was an orphan and a widow and had no relatives to take her in. The government promised her ..." Here I stopped and went rummaging in my notes to be sure I got the details right.

"First she went to her state government, Pennsylvania," I said. "And here's what the Council of Pennsylvania sent to the Board of War on June 29, 1789:

Ordered that the case of Margaret Corbin
who was wounded and utterly disabled at

Fort Washington, while she heroically filled
the post of her husband who was killed
by her side serving a piece of artillery, be
recommended to a further consideration of the
Board of War, this Council being of opinion,
that notwithstanding the rations which have
been allowed her, she is not provided for as
her helpless situation really requires.

"They gave her thirty dollars 'to relieve her present
necessities until her case can be provided for in a more
effectual manner.'"

"Thirty dollars doesn't sound like much," Greatgramps
said. "Would hardly buy you meals at McDonalds for a
week."

"Thirty dollars was a lot of money back then. Anyway,
she didn't have to wait a week," I said. "Government was
small in those days. The War Office and Congress were
right there in Philadelphia. So here's what came from the
War Office on July 3:

The enclosed communication of the Council
of Pennsylvania in favor of Margaret Corbin,
added to many circumstances which appear
to support her petition for relief, induces the
Board to offer a resolution which they think
her present situation merits. As she had
fortitude & virtue enough to supply the piece
of her husband after his fall in the service
of his country, and in the execution of that
task received the dangerous wound under
which she now labours, the Board can but
consider her as entitled to the same grateful

return which would be made to a soldier in circumstances equally unfortunate.

And Congress voted on this just three days later-on July 6

> *Resolved*, That Margaret Corbin, who was wounded and disabled in the attack on Fort Washington, whilst she heroically filled the post of her husband who was killed by her side serving a piece of artillery, do receive, during her natural life, or the continuance of the said disability, the one-half of the monthly pay drawn by a soldier in the service of these states; and that she now receive out of the public stores, one complete suit of cloaths [sic], or the value thereof in money.

So that was a promise right?" I said to Greatgramps.

"Can't get more official than an act of Congress," Greatgramps said. "So did they follow through on this?"

"Yes, but it wasn't enough. Especially not the clothes. A year later, July 24, 1780, the Board of War recommended another resolution that Congress passed:

> The board having received information that Margaret Corbin (for whom Congress made provision in their act of July 6, 1779 for her gallant conduct in serving a piece of artillery when her husband was killed by her side) still remains in a deplorable situation in consequence of her wound, by which she is deprived of the use of one arm, and is in other respects much

disabled and probably will continue a cripple during her life, Beg leave to report.

Resolved, That Margaret Corbin receive annually, during her natural life one compleat suit of cloaths out of the public stores, or the value thereof in money, in addition to the provision made for her by the act of Congress of July 6, 1779.

"Pretty good footnotes, don't you think?" I was proud of these documents—they didn't come from a book. Ms. Guelphstein's friend had gotten them from manuscripts in the Papers of the Continental Congress in the Library of Congress.

"Was that enough to take care of her?" Greatgramps asked. "You said she was homeless."

"They put her in the Invalid Corps, which was a unit for disabled veterans at West Point in New York. After sending them down to Philadelphia in wagons from Fort Washington, they must have reloaded the ones that didn't have homes to go to and sent them back north," I said.

"Typical," Greatgramps said. "How do you know Margaret Corbin was with them?"

"I found a book that lists the names of all the disabled soldiers assigned to the Invalid Corps. Margaret Corbin's name is there. She's the only woman on the list."

"Another impressive footnote," Greatgramps said, "and it limits your list of Molly Pitcher suspects. Given how harsh the life was, a lot of women who followed the army must have had physical problems. The government didn't feel responsible this way for any of the others."

"It wasn't fair, but that's how they did things in those days," I said. "Just as the officers got a lot more than regular soldiers after they were discharged, the women who were doing all that nursing and carrying water didn't get anything. Margaret Corbin got soldier's benefits because she was wounded in action while serving a weapon."

"You were saying that the government didn't follow through. What happened?"

"Well, for one thing the commissary up at West Point didn't give her the liquor ration all soldiers were supposed to get."

"Hah!" said Greatgramps. "I hope she didn't take that lying down."

"She didn't. She put in a claim to the War Department in September 1782 for all the liquor due her since January and got it authorized. But they spread the back payments over a period of time."

Greatgramps brushed his moustache. "That was probably wise," he said. "The war ended in 1783. What happened to the disabled soldiers then?"

"All of them were discharged. Here's the resolution Congress passed:

> *Resolved*, that the Corps of Invalids be reduced, such officers as have lost a limb or been completely disabled in service to retire on full pay for life; such officers as may not be included in this description to retire on the same principles with other officers of the army, such non-commissioned officers and soldiers as being strangers in the country and have been disabled in service are incapable of providing for their own subsistence and are proper subjects for a hospital, to be received into some field hospital to be appropriated

for the purpose and their support on such
provisions as may be hereafter determined,
to be entitled in the meantime to their
usual rations and clothing, and such non-
commissioned officers and soldiers in service
as may have homes to which they can retire
to be discharged on the principles of the
resolution of the 23rd of April last.

"So was Margaret Corbin sent to a hospital?"

"No. The hospitals kept records of patients and she's not on them. Actually, the last time her name is in a document is when she was complaining about not getting her liquor ration just before the end of the war."

"Is that the end of the story, then?"

"No, because the commissary at West Point still felt responsible for a disabled woman after the Invalid Corps disbanded. The officer there wrote letters to General Knox at the War Department about a woman he called Captain Molly. "

"Could that be someone other than Margaret Corbin?"

"I don't see how. Margaret Corbin was the only woman listed in the Invalid Corps."

Greatgramps nodded. "So she didn't go to a hospital. What became of her?"

"I can't find anything about the first couple of years, but in the fall of 1785 there's this letter." I went rummaging in my cards. "She must have been really sick because the officer writing says he needs to provide her with what he calls 'hospital stores,' and he's not sure she's going to live out the winter."

"But you said she wasn't in a hospital."

"She wasn't. They were trying to find a place for her to board in a private home. That probably wasn't so bad; women did most of the health care providing in those days, and the hospitals were pretty awful."

"Still are," Greatgramps muttered. I knew he couldn't wait to get out of the VA hospital after his heart attack.

"Anyway, there's this letter from September, 1785 saying, 'I have secured a place for Captain Molly till next Spring, if she should live so long.' But here's the sad part. Before the winter was over, he wrote another letter: 'I am at a loss what to do with Capt. Molly. She is such an offensive person that people are unwilling to take her in charge. This woman informs me she cannot keep her longer than the first of March, and I cannot [find] any [other] that is willing to keep her for that money and find her anything to eat and drink.'"

"So did she get thrown out in the snow?"

"No—at least not then. The woman she was staying with was a Mrs. Randalls, and she must have been a saint to put up with Captain Molly. The War Department wasn't offering her much money and was slow paying even what they promised her. Captain Molly lived through the winter, and a year later she was still hanging in there. Now here's the part that really makes me mad." I read from another card. "This is from April 1787. The officer at West Point writes to the War Office, 'I am informed by the woman that takes care of Capt. Molly, that she is much in want of Shifts.'"

"What are shifts?" Greatgramps asked.

I'd read enough of Alicia Spinnaker's historical romances to know the answer to that. "Shifts are what women wore as underwear in those days—sort of a long shirt that they wore under their petticoats and skirts. They didn't wear anything else under it. The shift was their nightgown too. If the Army was responsible for providing clothing for Captain Molly, the absolute least they should have given her was underwear."

"I agree," said Greatgramps. "But, you know, I've heard from some of the WAC vets over at the American Legion that getting underwear at the VA hospital was a problem for them. Some of those old gals say that they had to wear underwear made for men because there wasn't anything else."

"The War Office promised to send what she needed, but she was still waiting two months later. The officer at West Point wrote to General Knox to please expedite delivery of the shifts for Captain Molly, 'as she complains much for the want of them.' I should think she would complain!"

"Did she ever get them?" Greatgramps asked.

"I don't know, but that wasn't the only problem. A month after this letter about the shifts, the officer at West Point was reminding the War Office about the overdue rent. It seems Mrs. Randalls had never been paid for room and board for Captain Molly. Here's this letter dated August 13, 1787 saying the bill was outstanding since October 1785. I guess the War Office finally paid that, but in February, 1788 there was another letter saying the payments due Mrs. Randall were unpaid from June to November 1787."

"Did Mrs. Randall throw her out then?"

"I can't answer that," I said. "The last time she is mentioned in an official record is 1790. After that all there is is the oral history of a crazy old woman who used to hang around West Point wearing cast off pieces of soldier's clothing and insisting on being saluted as an officer. That ends with the tradition that she died in 1800 and was buried in Highland Falls, New York with a cedar sapling planted as a marker."

"That's a sad story," Greatgramps said. "I suppose no one ever put a decent marker over her. She sounds like she deserved one more than Mary Hays."

"She did get several markers eventually, though nothing near as fancy as what Mary Hays has. Some pictures are in that box we got from Mrs. Spinner. Her grave wasn't even identified for sure until 1926."

"How did that happen?"

"Well it seems there was a man who lived in Highland Falls who said that his grandfather had helped to bury Captain Molly and had pointed out the grave to his son. There was the stump of an old cedar tree there, and the man was sure it was the right place. Eventually the Daughters of the American Revolution took an interest and appointed a committee to study the evidence. The committee was convinced that the grave was that of Captain Molly and that Captain Molly had been Margaret Corbin. The DAR got permission to dig up the body and rebury it at West Point. The remains were moved to a grave in the United States Military Cemetery at West Point. This marker was dedicated on April 14, 1926." I'd found the picture in my file.

"It's good that Margaret Corbin was honored," Greatgramps said, "but could they be sure that the body they recovered was hers? Didn't you tell me some writers claimed she died and was buried in Pennsylvania?"

"I've got proof they were wrong," I said smugly, pulling out one of my prize note cards. "I've got forensic evidence."

Greatgramps's ears perked up at that. I told him how a surgeon from the West Point hospital had examined the skeleton before it was reburied and gave his opinion that it was "that of a female, and that the left shoulder bones bore evidence that they had been injured, verifying history that her shoulder and breast were badly bruised and battered."

Greatgramps nodded. You couldn't get evidence more solid than that.

"She may not have a huge display with a statue and a cannon," I said, "but Margaret Corbin was a real battlefield hero and is the only Revolutionary War veteran buried at West Point."

- fifteen -

Mrs. Spinner's Secret

Greatgramps and I went to call on Mrs. Spinner on Valentine's Day. She blushed when he gave her a box of chocolates in a red satin heart box and a bunch of yellow roses. He'd insisted I come along when he went "calling," but I felt silly as if I was supposed to be a chaperone. When I saw her blush I realized that both of them were shy, which struck me as beyond weird. Alicia Spinnaker knew the facts of life. Greatgramps knew them too; when his old buddies came to visit, I'd overheard them telling some really raunchy stories about sneaking out of barracks to seduce WACs and nurses in the South Pacific. I was sure most of them were pure fantasy, and maybe that was the trouble. Alicia Spinnaker's stories were fantasy too.

Mrs. Spinner served tea and some little cakes with pink icing and we handed around the box of chocolates. Greatgramps praised the cakes, Mrs. Spinner praised the roses, they interrupted each other to comment on the weather, and then both of them looked at me.

Mrs. Spinner glanced at Greatgramps and they locked eyes.

"Peggy, can you keep a secret," Mrs. Spinner asked. I noticed that she did not call me Miss Peggy. I nodded and noticed Greatgramps grinning at me. Mrs. Spinner was going to confess the secret of her double identity.

"Come then," she said. "You stay here, Patrick," she added. "There's not room in the shed for more than two people."

"If I must," said Greatgramps. "Can I look through your Civil War collection while I wait?"

"Of course. But mind your fingers are clean if you handle any of the older volumes. I don't want pink icing on Grant's memoirs."

Leaving Greatgramps in the house, Mrs. Spinner took a big key from a hook by the back door and led me out across the yard to one of the outbuildings. There were several on her property. One was an outhouse no longer in use because even in her most early American moods, Mrs. Spinner appreciated indoor plumbing. Another structure housed Fluffy and his friends. Mrs. Spinner headed for what looked like a woodshed with heaps of logs piled along one side. Then I saw there was a door at the end of the building. Mrs. Spinner opened it with her key and I blinked in amazement.

"This is where I write," she said.

The door opened into a modern room painted white with a pale pink floor. The whole wall facing the door was glass looking out into the woods and a skylight was set into the roof. The room was nearly as bright as if we were still outdoors. I could see recessed fixtures in the ceiling and a lamp stood on an enormous desk in front of the window, but except at night or in very bad weather it would always be light enough to write in that room.

Angled in a corner next to the desk was a stand with a computer and a printer. A comfortable looking chair on wheels upholstered in dark red leather with brass studs could move from the desk to the computer and around the floor to the shelves of books that covered the walls on the long sides of the room. On one side the shelves held reference books, while on the other side they were entirely filled with books in bright paper covers that identified them as Alicia Spinnaker novels.

"I see you recognize them," Mrs. Spinner said. "Mr. McAllister said you were a fan."

"Are you a Spinnaker fan too?" I asked, acting innocent until I was sure she meant to share that secret. She might just have been showing me that she didn't always live in rooms with hardwood floors and candles.

"It's worse than that," she said. "I am Alicia Spinnaker."

"Really?" I said trying to sound amazed. "Why that's wonderful. The author's note in all your books says 'Alicia Spinnaker lives in seclusion in New Jersey' and never shows a photo. And here you live right here in Lindwood. Wow!"

"You won't tell anyone, will you?" Mrs. Spinner sounded concerned as if I might really break my promise and tell her secret.

"No," I said. "Not anyone. Not even Greatgramps."

Mrs. Spinner laughed. "Oh it is all right to talk to your greatgrandfather. He figured out my secret years ago. But the reason I wanted to show this room to you is so you could see how I work. My contract says I have to write two books a year, so I have learned to be very efficient.

You have collected an impressive stack of research notes, but now you have only a few weeks to put them into order. How do you plan to go about writing your paper?" Mrs. Spinner sat down in the leather chair and motioned me to a recliner next to a book-strewn table. I glanced enviously at Mrs. Spinner's computer.

"I'll make an outline—I have to do that as an assignment. Then I'll organize the note cards I need so they are in the order of the outline. Then I'll write one section at a time on Greatgramps's yellow lined pads, and when it's all done, I'll type it up on the electric typewriter my Mom had when she was in college.

"Isn't there a computer you can use at school?" Mrs. Spinner asked.

"Not really," I said. "There are computers in the school library, but you have a time limit when you use them."

"I've seen that box of notes you've collected, Peggy. How many pages do you think you will be writing?"

I hadn't thought about that. I'd never had an assignment like this one before. For once Mr. Pettibone had not set a maximum length, just a minimum: fifteen double-spaced pages. I knew I would end up with more than that. Probably a lot more.

Mrs. Spinner got up from her chair and opened a cupboard that held office supplies. She reached into the bottom shelf and pulled out what looked like a large notebook.

"Here," she said. You can borrow this. Save the file on disk and all you will need to do at school is print it out."

I took the object she handed me, not knowing what to say. It was a laptop computer in a leather case.

"I used to take that with me when I went on research trips," she said, "but now I use this instead." She reached into a bag stitched together like a patchwork quilt and pulled out a tiny handheld computer with a little folding keyboard. "Now I take this with me," she said. "That laptop you're holding seemed to me like the ultimate in technology when I got it three years ago."

It still seemed pretty ultimate to me. I was still adjusting to the idea of Mrs. Spinner having this secret modern life out behind her colonial house.

"Now we'd better go back inside," Mrs. Spinner said. "I don't want Mr. McAllister to think I've forgotten about him."

We walked back toward the house, Mrs. Spinner holding her patchwork bag and me carrying the laptop. I could scarcely believe it. Not only did I have a computer, but one that had been used by a famous writer.

"We have returned, Mr. McAllister," Mrs. Spinner announced as she entered the parlor. Greatgramps stood up and put down the book he'd been reading.

Mrs. Spinner returned to her rocking chair by the fire and took her knitting from her bag. I stood clutching the laptop to my chest so excited I didn't want to sit down.

- sixteen -
The Detective's Summation

"This might be an appropriate time for the detective's summation," Greatgramps said.

"I had the same thought, Mr. McAllister," Mrs. Spinner replied.

"What's a 'detective's summation?'" I asked.

"You've read Agatha Christie, Peg." Greatgramps said. "Remember how at the end of the story, the great detective calls everyone together and gives a speech explaining the steps by which he solved the case."

"Another way to imagine it is the way a lawyer sums up his case for the jury," Mrs. Spinner added. "We will be the audience. Tell us what you intend to say in your paper."

"Just like that? Here? Now? But I don't have my note cards."

"Just wing it," said Greatgramps. "We're listening."

I felt a sudden rush of excitement. I could do this! I put the laptop down and stood in front of the fire with my hands behind my back feeling like the great detective.

"We are presented with two questions," I began. "Was there a Molly Pitcher and who was she? But we must first answer a third question: What was Molly Pitcher?"

Greatgramps and Mrs. Spinner were both listening attentively.

"Molly Pitcher is more than a woman on the front lines during the American Revolution. There were many of those." I quoted from memory from the 1822 newspaper article Ms. Guelphstein gave me for Christmas. "It was not an unusual circumstance to find women in the ranks disguised as men, such was their ardor for independence."

"I never heard of anyone but Molly Pitcher," said Greatgramps scowling and leaning back with his arms crossed, playing the skeptic.

"For example," I said, picking up the cue. "In addition to my Molly Pitcher suspects, two women held pensions based on military service: Deborah Samson who enlisted late in the war and Anna Marie Lane who was wounded at the Battle of Germantown. There is a report of a woman serving a cannon at Fort Clinton and a woman relieving her husband at an infantry position at the battle of Monmouth. None of these, however, fill the requirements for the role of Molly Pitcher," I concluded dramatically and did some pacing back and forth in front of the fire trying to look like Hercule Poirot. Greatgramps put his hand to his mouth to hide his grin.

"What, you may ask, are those requirements?" Now I was grinning, conscious of stealing one of Mr. Pettibone's tricks. "They are these: One, Molly Pitcher must have fought at the Battle of Monmouth. Two, she must have had a husband serving in artillery who was killed in that action. Three, she must have carried water to soldiers during that action, and four, she must have taken her husband's place serving at an artillery piece, either loading or firing the weapon."

"If I may," Mrs. Spinner raised her hand. I nodded pompously the way Mr. Pettibone does giving her permission to speak. "Why do you insist on these four points? All of the recent books about Molly Pitcher have her husband merely wounded or even simply dropping from exhaustion."

"Ah, hah!" I exclaimed locking one arm behind my back and raising my forefinger. "Yes! Those recent books. They changed the story and that is why there is a mystery. All of the earliest accounts of the events at Monmouth agree that the woman at the cannon replaced a man who had been instantly killed." I ticked them off on my fingers. "George Washington Custis says killed, Benjamin Lossing says killed, Dr. Thatcher says killed. All of them say killed. As late as 1896, the collection of folklore of New Jersey tells of a man named Pitcher at the gun battery at the Battle of Monmouth whose wife brought him water and took over his position after he was killed by a bullet."

"When did the story change?" Greatgramps asked on cue.

"Not so much when did it change," I replied, "but where." I did a bit of pacing in front of the fire, then swiveled to confront my audience dramatically. "As I have just mentioned, in New Jersey, in the neighborhood of the battle, the story continued to include a husband who was killed until the end of the nineteenth century, but in a town in Pennsylvania many miles from the action, it was changed."

"Carlisle," Mrs. Spinner volunteered helpfully.

"Exactly. In Carlisle, Pennsylvania, in 1876, the year of the centennial of the Revolution, a local woman named Mary Hays was identified by members of a patriotic organization as the real Molly Pitcher and a marker with that fact carved into solid stone was placed on that woman's grave."

"Well surely that proves something," Mrs. Spinner suggested. "Such an expensive marker would not have been placed if the story had been entirely made up."

"But, you see, not all of it was made up. Only the one tiny detail was changed. The Molly Pitcher of Carlisle was not widowed during the war."

"Madam Detective," Greatgramps raised his hand. "I recall you telling me in previous conversations that there is more than one error on that marker. The name of the husband was wrong and the age at death was wrong."

"True," I replied, "but these are minor errors, genealogical errors. The key error is the surviving husband, since all earlier sources agree that the real Molly Pitcher was a widow."

"If Mrs. Hays carried water and fired a cannon at the Battle of Monmouth, I'd be willing to recognize her as Molly Pitcher," Greatgramps replied stubbornly.

"But there is no certain evidence that she did that either," I said. "I will concede the probability that she carried water for swabbing the cannon on that day. Her husband was enrolled in Proctor's artillery and his unit did fight at Monmouth. His wife followed him during the war, and if he was there it is probable that she was too. Carrying water to the cannon was women's work. So it is probable, although not certain, that she carried water. But it is a long way from that to have her loading or firing a cannon."

"Then who was the woman who fired the cannon at the Battle of Monmouth?" Mrs. Spinner asked.

"Patience, patience," I said. This master detective role was starting to feel really comfortable. Maybe if I didn't grow up to be a detective or librarian I could be an actress. "Before I examine that question, we must consider the cases of the women who fired weapons at Fort Clinton and Fort Washington." My audience subsided and looked at me expectantly.

"The woman at Fort Clinton is a very murky figure. Benjamin Lossing said that the woman who fired the last shot at that battle was the same woman who fired on the enemy at the Battle of Monmouth, but that appears to have been merely an assumption on his part. By contrast, the woman at Fort Washington, Margaret Corbin, is solidly documented. She fits three of the four requirements for the Molly Pitcher role: as a soldier's wife she may be presumed to have carried water, her husband was killed in action, and she served at the cannon after he fell."

"But she was at the wrong battle," Greatgramps said.

"And she was not called Molly Pitcher," I added. "She was always referred to as Captain Molly."

"Then there were two artillery heroines," Mrs. Spinner suggested. "Margaret Corbin was Captain Molly and the woman at Monmouth was Molly Pitcher."

"It's not quite that simple," I said. "The woman at the Battle of Monmouth is called Captain Molly in all of the early accounts."

"Could the two stories have been confused? Could both have been referring to the same person?"

"It's possible, but Margaret Corbin's story does not seem to have been clearly remembered. Even in her lifetime, an officer administering her pension at West Point thought she had been rewarded for service at Brandywine." I suddenly made another connection. "Brandywine is the battle where Mary Hays was believed to have been wounded."

"What does that prove?" Greatgramps asked.

"Nothing, I guess, except that some woman was wounded at Brandywine. It couldn't have been Margaret Corbin. She was disabled in November of 1776 and Brandywine was fought a year later."

"A novelist might make something of the connection," Mrs. Spinner said. "But of course that wouldn't be history."

"I'm still waiting to hear about Molly Pitcher," Greatgramps said. "When does she come in?"

"Molly Pitcher doesn't come in until 1848 when Nathaniel Currier uses the name on a print. The first time that name is used in a book is in 1859 when Benjamin Lossing edited George Washington Parke Custis's *Memoirs of Washington*. He wrote in a footnote about the woman at Monmouth that 'Art and Romance have confounded her with another character, Moll Pitcher.' Both Custis and Lossing call the woman Captain Molly and so does everyone else until 1862."

After all this talking, I was getting thirsty. I retrieved my empty teacup and held it out to Mrs. Spinner for a refill.

"I wonder if that 'character' was Moll Pitcher of Lynn," Mrs. Spinner mused.

"What happened in 1862?" Greatgramps asked as I sipped my tea.

"At that point the 'confounding' of the two characters seems to have taken permanent hold. In 1862 a new edition was published of a Revolutionary War classic. Dr. James Thatcher published his wartime journal in 1823.

It was republished in 1827 and again in 1854, ten years after Thatcher's death. In the fourth edition, published in 1862 an entirely new section was inserted into the entry for July 4, 1778 when Thatcher recorded what he had heard about the Battle fought at Monmouth Court House a few days earlier. The new section describes the actions of 'Molly Pitcher, wife of one of the officers.'"

"An officer's wife?" asked Greatgramps

"That's what the book says. The story includes the business of her being on half-pay as an officer for life and being 'ever afterward called Capt. Molly.'"

"Well that doesn't sound at all like the poor homeless woman known as Captain Molly up in New York."

"No it doesn't. And more than that, in his entry for July 30, 1779, just a few weeks after Congress voted a pension for Margaret Corbin, Dr. Thatcher wrote about that in his journal and quoted the text of the resolution without calling her Captain Molly. The editors of the 1862 edition of the journal who inserted the Molly Pitcher material didn't make any connection. Fourteen years later, the alleged real Mary Pitcher turns up buried in Carlisle."

"I've been thinking about that," Greatgramps said. "I'm remembering the eyewitness account by Martin published in 1830 of the woman at Monmouth whose petticoat was torn away while she served at a cannon. Her husband was not killed. Could she have been Mary Hays? Even without the rest of the details being true, wouldn't that be close enough?"

"I'm sure it would be close enough for the people in Carlisle," Mrs. Spinner said. "After more than a century, no one is going to take down any monuments. But I see why Peggy must remain skeptical." Now Mrs. Spinner started ticking off points on her fingers. "One, there is no reason to connect the petticoat story with the taking-over-the-cannon story. The versions circulating in New Jersey and recorded by early writers never mention it even though the Custis version includes a conversation between Molly and General Washington where her petticoats are discussed. Custis had a perfect opening, but apparently he had never heard the story. Two, and this is a telling point to me, Mary Hays's obituary notices say nothing about the Battle of Monmouth even though by the time she died the folk history of Captain Molly was well established. Three, the indirect evidence that would connect Mary Hays to the woman with the damaged petticoat would equally as well apply to any artilleryman's wife at the battle."

"What about her pension?" Greatgramps said. "That proves she was special."

"Yes," I broke in. "Special for service as a soldier at Brandywine."

We sat in silence for a minute. I had run out of steam and my great detective had hit a dead end.

"Was there a Molly Pitcher?" Greatgramps asked finally.

The great detective was now on the spot. I took a deep breath and committed myself. "At the time of the Revolution there was no woman known as Molly Pitcher. There was a woman known as Captain Molly, but she was not at the Battle of Monmouth. There were many brave women on battlefields of the American Revolution, and after the war there was a strong desire to remember female heroism. So what I believe is that the spirit of Molly Pitcher was real but no single person embodied that spirit."

"Sort of like Santa Claus and Saint Nicholas," Greatgramps summed up.

"Maybe, but there is no way I am going to put that in my paper."

"Very wise of you, Miss Peggy," Mrs. Spinner said putting away her knitting. "A description of the spirit of Molly Pitcher will make a much stronger conclusion." I heard something click as Mrs. Spinner reached into her bag. She pulled out a tape recorder and ejected the tape. "Take this," she said handing it to me. "You have quite eloquently blocked out your whole paper. All you need to do now is add footnotes."

seventeen

Fact and Fiction

The laptop computer made creating an outline for my paper really easy. I played around with all the different choices for formatting before settling for something ordinary enough to keep Mr. Pettibone from criticizing. The next step was the footnotes, and although Mrs. Spinner talked as if that was the easy part, I knew it wouldn't be. I'd checked out enough footnotes from the history books and articles I'd studied to know that even the best writers could get page numbers or dates of publication wrong. Mrs. Spinner's spellcheck program wouldn't help me if I made mistakes like that.

I went to the library and checked out the books from the children's section again so I could study them more closely. When I first looked at them, I was just frustrated because they contradicted each other, and I couldn't tell what was real and what was made up. Now that I knew more about where the story came from, I could tell where the author was sticking with the oldest traditions and where a new creative twist had been added to the story.

For instance Gleiter and Thompson's *Molly Pitcher* has a dramatic scene at the end. The battle is over and the sun has set. Molly falls to the ground, exhausted, and is carried from the field while two other men, one of them with a bandage around his head, help her husband John. There is no proof that such a thing happened, and no one ever mentioned it before. But it is the sort of thing that could have happened.

I leaned back, closed my eyes and made up a scene of my own for the night following the battle. I thought of George Washington, wrapped in his cloak on the battlefield, too worked up to sleep. He was angry at General Charles Lee for disobeying orders and worried about the British army coming back in the morning. Maybe his aide, who I remembered had been Alexander Hamilton, couldn't sleep either and brought the general something to drink. They talked a few minutes under the stars. I smiled to myself. I liked that scene. It wasn't history, but it made George Washington seem more human, and it didn't contradict anything the history books could prove.

Making up plausible stories that fit inside historical events was what Alicia Spinnaker did. When I read her stories I had a feeling of really knowing the past that I never got from the serious history books.

When the first Captain Molly stories appeared in print, the authors were giving their version of local oral histories. People told the stories to each other and elaborated on them so there would have been dozens of versions by the time Custis or Lossing wrote theirs down. I once read a book about fairy tales that gave examples of how stories like Cinderella changed as different people repeated them. Knowing what I did now about Molly Pitcher, I believed that her story had grown just like Cinderella's and could have gone on growing and changing forever except for Custis and Lossing publishing versions that were presented as genuine historical fact.

I looked at my note cards from Custis and Lossing. There were some quotations, but the authors of the books I copied those from had only put in bits and pieces. Teachers said it was poor style to use a lot of long quotations, which is probably why the authors I read hadn't used them. But with only bits and pieces, how could I be sure that they interpreted the story the way I would? Or even that they had copied them correctly. I'd found several books that made mistakes copying that I'd never have known about if I hadn't checked back to the original primary source.

I knew just what I wanted from Custis and Lossing and Thatcher and a few other really old books that had been the earliest to talk about Captain Molly or Molly Pitcher at Monmouth. I even knew the pages the stories were on. But they weren't in the Lindwood Public Library, and Ms. Guelphstein wasn't able to get interlibrary loan librarians to make xerox copies because they were too old and fragile. I walked home from the library feeling frustrated.

When I got back home, I was surprised to find Mrs. Spinner sitting in our living room drinking tea. Somehow I had thought that she never left her early American home and would suddenly vanish if she tried to move out into the real world. Such things happened in fairy tales, and the description of Alicia Spinnacker "living in seclusion" suggested something similar.

Greatgramps had set up a TV dinner table in the living room with a teapot, a little pitcher of milk, and a plate of cookies. I almost laughed to see our everyday mugs and plates on a rickety metal table imitating the antique piecrust tea table and bone china that Mrs. Spinner used in her parlor.

"Mrs. Spinner is paying us a call," Greatgramps announced in a dignified voice. "Would you care to join us in a light afternoon repast?"

"Milk and cookies would be most welcome," I said. "Please do not trouble yourself to bring them. I shall help myself and join you with all deliberate speed."

Greatgramps raised an eyebrow at my combination of early American and law court vocabulary, but Mrs. Spinner nodded at me benevolently.

I brought my snack into the living room on a tray and sat on the floor. I thought it wise not to test the capacity of the TV table.

"I am making a short research trip down to Washington," Mrs. Spinner announced, setting her cup down neatly, "and your greatgrandfather has been kind enough to offer to escort me to the thirtieth street train station."

"I brought her back here for tea first," said Greatgramps grinning. "Thought you might like to come along for the ride."

I was getting a bit big to go riding in the back seat of the Volkswagen, but I was willing to squeeze myself in. I'd have the front seat on the ride home.

"Sure," I said. "What are you researching, Mrs. Spinner?"

Mrs. Spinner blushed. "Oh, a little bit of this and that," she said. "I might branch out a little in researching my family history. And I've thought of preparing a monograph on the place of Lindwood in George Washington's strategic planning for the New Jersey campaigns. There was a rather notorious loyalist living on what is now Broad Street. It was rumored that his wife had a connection with Peggy Shippen Arnold."

"Benedict Arnold's wife?" I said. "What a great story! Where will you go to find evidence about that?"

"Oh, I always go to the main library at DAR headquarters," Mrs. Spinner said. "What they don't have, they can find for me. The staff there knows me from way back." She blushed again. "From before I was Alicia Spinnaker."

"I wish I could use a library like that," I said.

"That reminds me," Mrs. Spinner said, reaching into her patchwork bag and taking out her tiny computer. "I was going to ask you if there is anything you'd like me to pick up for you while I am down there."

"You mean they'd let you take books out?" I asked

"Oh, no," she said. "I can't do that. But if you have some reference that you'd like me to check on, I can do that. I won't do research for you," she added sternly, "that would be cheating. But if you have titles and page numbers, I can be a file clerk and make copies."

I grinned broadly and got my index cards from my backpack. "Well it just so happens I could use a few things," I said.

- eighteen -
Speculations on
Drinking and Nudity

"I've been thinking about the Battle of Monmouth," I said. It was Easter Sunday, and we were having a family dinner with Mrs. Spinner as our guest.

"Why am I not surprised," Mom said, and everybody laughed.

"Sorry, honey," Mom said. "I shouldn't have said that."

"That's okay," I said. "I know I'm a monomaniac."

"She always uses such big words," Mom said to Mrs. Spinner apologetically.

Mrs. Spinner smiled and nodded at my mother and then spoke to me in her best eighteenth century manner. "Pray tell, Miss Peggy. Of what in particular have you been thinking? I must confess, though not a monomaniac, that I have long been fascinated by that memorable event in our nation's history."

"Thanks," I said, trying not to laugh while imitating her way of speaking. "If I have permission to pursue this line of conversation, I'd like to ask Greatgramps a question."

"About the Battle of Monmouth?" Greatgramps looked startled "Everything I know about that I heard from you."

"It's not so much that particular battle. I'm thinking more in general about how soldiers behave in combat," I said.

"I can talk about World War II and Korea," Greatgramps said. "But I don't know if what we did then applies for any other war."

"Well, just suppose," I said. "I can't ask a Revolutionary War veteran."

"That's true," Greatgramps said. "What do you want to know?"

"I'm wondering whether during combat soldiers might decide not to obey orders," I said. Greatgramps had been sipping his wine and trying to look like an elegant gentleman for Mrs. Spinner. My question took him by surprise and wine sloshed on the tablecloth.

"Peggy," he said, trying to wipe up the mess unobtrusively with his napkin. "Disobeying orders while under fire will get you shot. And I don't mean by the enemy; it's a capital offense."

"I don't mean disobeying big orders," I said. "Just little ones. Like ones about hygiene or dress codes, for instance."

"Like drug use," Mom said.

"Yes, exactly!" I said. "I remember Grandpa Bill telling me that there was a lot of pot smoking in Vietnam. It was against the rules, and the doctors said it was very dangerous, but when soldiers were in the field under stress they smoked it anyway."

Grandpa Bill was Mom's dad. He'd come home from Vietnam and lived to tell stories. I never knew my Grandpa Mike; Greatgramps's son had died incountry.

"If you're talking about things like that, then I have to confess that my buddies and I did not always follow every letter of the rules and regulations," Greatgramps said. "What is this leading up to Peggy?"

"Two things," I said. "One is the whole business about Molly Pitcher bringing water to the soldiers. A book I read quoted from a pamphlet by a doctor named Benjamin Rush about how to preserve the health of soldiers. The War Office had it printed for the officers of the Continental Army. Dr. Rush described the symptoms and treatment for something called 'cold water disease.'"

"Peggy," my mother interrupted. "This may not be an appropriate topic for dinner table conversation."

"Oh, pray let her continue," Mrs. Spinner interrupted. "I have always been fascinated by the medical practices of the olden days. And Dr. Rush was such an influential man in his time. Rather odd when you think back on it since he was so enthusiastic about bleeding his patients. Some of his prescriptions called for bleeding out more blood than there is in a human body."

Mrs. Spinner's comment being even less suitable for dinner table conversation than what I had in mind, I felt encouraged to plough ahead.

"Dr. Rush said cold water disease was caused by drinking water colder than body temperature. Soldiers served water were supposed to hold the cup in their hands until it warmed up. If they were overheated they were not supposed to drink water at all. If they did, within a few minutes they would have trouble breathing and then collapse. They'd be dead within five minutes unless someone got to them with a dose of laudanum. That's a form of opium."

"I don't know about the laudanum, but the symptoms of cold water disease sound like heat stroke. That's definitely a medical emergency," Greatgramps said. "What you need is ice; pack it under the victim's arms to get his temperature down. We'd call for a medic to evacuate. They'd get the victim into ice water. When the heat's got to someone so bad that they lose consciousness, you certainly would not try to pour water down their throats. The medics would use IVs to hydrate."

"Well my question is what did the Revolutionary soldiers do? They didn't have any ice and they couldn't get into any shade unless they left the battlefield. Did they obey the officers who told them not to drink water until the battle was over and they had time to cool down? Or did they do what their bodies must have wanted which was to drink as much water as they could get? It wasn't just Dr. Rush who believed drinking cold water could kill you—not that any water would be that cold on such a hot day unless it was fresh out of a deep well. Dr. Thatcher said sixty or eighty men on both sides died at Monmouth from heat, exhaustion, and drinking cold water."

"He underestimated," said Mrs. Spinner. "More than five hundred British soldiers died of heat stroke during the Battle of Monmouth."

"Why would Molly Pitcher have been carrying water to the soldiers if the officers thought it would kill them?" Mom asked.

"The women of the army were not carrying water for drinking," I said, "The early drawings show Molly Pitcher with a wooden bucket, the kind used to hold water to swab out the cannon to cool it between shots."

"I imagine someone dying of thirst, with his tongue swollen as soldiers are described at the Battle of Monmouth, might dip into one of those cannonier's buckets if he could reach one," Mrs. Spinner said. "But most soldiers were infantry, not artillery."

"If Molly Pitcher was running around bringing them water to drink, wouldn't the officers think she was trying to kill the soldiers rather than do a good deed? Or were they all pretty skeptical of Dr. Rush's advice and would take a drink themselves if they could?"

"Just speaking from my own experience," Greatgramps said, "I think I'd obey the doctor. There are battlefield wounds that are made worse if you give the guy anything to drink. At least that's what the medics told us, and I did believe the medics. Trying to give water to someone who is unconscious or for some other reason can't swallow is obviously a bad idea. Something you haven't mentioned is the danger of drinking water that isn't clean. What was used to swab the cannon was pretty filthy. The officers would want to protect the soldiers from that too."

"If patients allowed Dr. Rush to bleed them to death, they'd probably accept the 'no water when overheated' rule too," Mrs. Spinner said. "At least that is my guess."

"That brings me to my second question," I said. "This is something I got from one of the library books. In *They Called Her Molly Pitcher* the author said that the British soldiers wore their heavy uniforms but the Americans knew about hot, humid New Jersey weather. So even though they had spent all winter drilling with von Steuben so they would look and act like European soldiers, when it started to heat up at Monmouth, they ignored the rules about looking neat and military. She says 'They stripped off coats, belts, wigs, hats, boots, shoes, and stockings and tossed them onto the grass.' Ordinary soldiers didn't have wigs, so that would mean that even the officers were stripping down to their knee britches."

Greatgramps roared. "Did someone really write that? Megan, do you remember that old Alan Alda film called *Sweet Liberty*?" he asked my mother.

"Oh, yes, the one about the college professor who writes a history book and sells the screen rights." Mom said.

"I remember that one too," said Mrs. Spinner. "It was about the southern campaign I seem to recall. In the movie the film director and the actors didn't like the real history of the battle and insisted on changing it all around, making the monstrous Banastre Tarleton into a kindly romantic figure, and at the end—oh, yes, at the end the professor got his revenge." Mrs. Spinner started to laugh

"At the end of the film all the reenactors playing the part of American militia take off all their clothes." Greatgramps said.

"Yes, I remember that." Mon broke in. "They tore off absolutely everything and threw shirts and hats and pants into the air. It was hilarious."

"We'll have to rent the video sometime so Peggy can see it," Greatgramps said.

"So does that mean you don't think soldiers would really take their clothes off—at least their hats and their shirts—during a battle even if it was really hot?" I asked.

"Absolutely not," said Mrs. Spinner. "For one thing it isn't true that clothing makes one hotter. Natural fibers like wool are good insulation, which is why people in desert climes wear robes that cover them completely. And even today people know they should wear hats when out in the hot sun. Besides, the soldiers knew how important it was to look like a real army. If they had taken their shirts off,

135

the British would confirm their belief that the Americans were undisciplined savages."

"Regular redskins," Greatgramps added, "because there'd have been some really bad cases of sunburn among men who weren't used to it going shirtless."

"Of course the Americans did not have much clothing to begin with," Mrs. Spinner said. "Full uniform for the British involved more layers of clothing and heavy packs, so in that respect they would have been more vulnerable to heat stroke than the Americans."

"Thank you," I said. "I'm used to the idea of the American soldiers barefoot and in rags, but I didn't at all like the idea of them undressing in the face of the enemy."

- nineteen -
Out of My Hands

By Easter my paper was practically finished. Using Mrs. Spinner's computer was a terrific help. Not only did it correct my spelling and grammar mistakes, but it also let me put in additions and corrections without having to retype everything.

I had never done a paper with footnotes before and had wondered how I would make the notes come out right at the bottom of the page if I'd had to use my Mom's old electric typewriter. With the computer, I just had to click on "Insert" and the footnote would come in at the right place with the right number attached.

I always get my assignments done early because I hate feeling pressured. The Rattletop paper was due on Friday; I had it finished by Tuesday. It was long. If I'd had more time I could have made it shorter. I talked about that with Mrs. Spinner, and she said she had the same problem. The first drafts of her books were always much longer than the published version. Knowing how to cut, she told me, is an important skill for a writer. Unfortunately, Mr. Pettibone's assignment schedule didn't leave time for editing.

The further along I got on my paper, the more nervous I'd been about the file somehow getting erased. I backed up the work every day on two disks. I left one in the computer and put the other in my backpack in case there was a fire and I had to climb out my bedroom window in the middle of the night. On the Tuesday before the due date, I ran spell check one last time and compared my long quotations with the xeroxes Mrs. Spinner had brought me, and the next day I took the disk to the school library to print it out on the computer.

Mr. Pettibone said that those of us who wanted our papers to be considered for the Rattletop Award had to submit six copies: one for him to grade and five for the committee of judges. On the copies for judges we were to put just the title of the paper without our names. Mr. Pettibone would randomly select numbers for each of us that would be a secret identification mark. That way, he said, none of the judges would know who we were. They wouldn't even know if the author was a boy or a girl. Of course Mr. Pettibone would know. I wondered why they let teachers grade students when they could be prejudiced even though it wasn't allowed for judges.

No one was on line to use the computer. This late in the term all the students who had computers at home were using those, so I put in my disk and brought up the file. For some stupid reason I'd been afraid it wouldn't work, but there it was just as I had it on Mrs. Spinner's laptop. I gave a sigh of relief and hit File and Print.

Just as I got going, the printer's light started flashing "toner low." I paused the printing and went to get the librarian. Then I started up again, but I was only about halfway through the first copy when the printer ran out of paper. The librarian opened another ream, and I started printing again.

After a while the librarian came to check on me even though there was no one else on line. She asked how I was coming along and I said I was doing fine. Then the printer ran out of paper again. She looked annoyed and asked me just how long my paper was. I told her it was 139 pages including the bibliography. She did the math in her head and told me the school could not afford to give a single student that much paper, not to mention the toner. She said to stop the printer and take my disk somewhere else to finish.

I hadn't figured on having this kind of problem. But I still had another day to go, so I took the disk home and asked Greatgramps what I should do. After everything she'd done for me already, I didn't want to ask Mrs. Spinner. Greatgramps went into his contacts file and found a friend who owned a print shop. After a phone call, he told me he'd made a deal to do an oil change and a tune-up on his friend's antique Edsel in return for six copies of a 139 page paper. Recycle what I'd done so far, he said, because his friend would do something that looked much more professional.

All that was fine, but when I got home from school Thursday afternoon, Greatgramps said my paper hadn't been printed yet. His friend, after all, had a business to run. Just as I was about to have hysterics he told me that it was all right. His friend would be working late and promised that the paper would be ready early Friday morning. My social studies class didn't meet until after lunch, so I could come home and pick it up and turn it in on time.

I hated having to cut it so tight, but I trusted Greatgramps and, of course, he came through for me. When I came home for lunch on Friday, I was almost too excited to eat. The printer had done my Rattletop report on two sides of the paper so it looked like a real book with a spiral binding and clear plastic covers on the front and back. The six copies were packed in a carton with the copy for Mr. Pettibone on top. I was so afraid of being late for social studies class that I got back to school ten minutes early.

That was how I happened to be passing the teachers' lounge and overheard a conversation that was not meant for my ears.

"I'd say it's your own fault, Mark. Why did you put off asking the Rattletop judge for so long?" I recognized the voice of Mrs. Cornwall, the English teacher.

"I wanted to make sure the name was kept a secret." That was Mr. Pettibone. "If the students knew who the history judge was, some would attempt to win the award by brown-nosing."

"I think that's unlikely." That was Mr. Youngblood, the science teacher.

"You're entitled to your opinion, Ralph," Mr. Pettibone snapped, "but it was my responsibility. If the school board had just let the social studies teacher decide on the winner, I wouldn't have had these problems."

"So now at the last minute you've gone and asked our famous local historian, and she's turned you down." Mr. Youngblood sounded amused.

"Citing a conflict of interest," Mr. Pettibone snapped back again. "That shows that some student did try to influence her vote."

"Before she was even asked to be a judge? Come off it, Mark. You want us to believe you've got some little Machiavelli in your class? Isn't it more likely Mrs. Spinner has a grandchild or some niece or nephew with a kid in your class."

"No!" snapped Mr. Pettibone—who was doing a lot of snapping. "Mrs. Spinner never had any children and has no living relatives. Her husband, George Hamilton Spinner, was the last of his line, and he died fifty years ago. Mrs. Spinner is the last of the Von Kleerks, which you would know if you had any knowledge of the history of this town," he said with what sounded like a sneer.

I gulped as I took all this in. Mr. Pettibone had asked Mrs. Spinner to be a judge for the Rattletop Award, and she had refused. It had to be because of me. And Mr. Pettibone thought it was because some student had been trying to influence her vote. Part of me felt like running to the girls' room and bawling. Another part of me wanted to know how the argument in the teachers' lounge would come out.

"Simmer down, Mark," Mrs. Cornwall broke in. "Surely there are other people you can ask to be Rattletop judge."

"Of course there are. That twit Carl Harrison who is head of social studies over at Lindwood Community College would love to be a judge. Put it on his resume along with all his other so-called scholarly credentials. A Ph.D. by distance learning of all things."

"Those of us without Ph.D.s of any kind should, perhaps, not judge him too harshly for that," Mrs. Cornwall said softly.

"Most of the votes will still come from the politicians anyway, won't they? All the school board members accepted didn't they? I don't see why you're so riled up about the local historian vote," Mr. Youngblood said.

"Because none of the politicians know anything about history. They'll automatically vote for an essay on someone they know. Without having one person who knows some history on the panel to focus their discussion, the competition will end up being a popularity contest. The Democrats will all vote for a John Kennedy paper, and the Republicans will all vote for Ronald Reagan."

"My, my. Are those the people your students consider great American heroes? I'd have thought they'd go for military figures," Mr. Youngblood said.

"Actually, most of them have," said Mr. Pettibone. "I was just giving an example."

Suddenly the bell rang. I tore down the hall with the carton of papers in my arms and was the first student seated for social studies class.

Mr. Pettibone arrived in a bad mood. Only I knew why. He told the students who were competing for the Rattletop Award to pass their six copies in first, and when he saw how many there were he complained about students who knew they had no chance of winning wasting everyone's time by insisting on having their work read. When I turned in my work in a carton he really went ballistic.

"Peggy, do you do things like this just to annoy me? I have twenty of these things to grade, and yours is as long as all the others combined." He dropped the carton on the floor and piled the other papers on top of it.

I knew better than to argue. I wondered if Mr. Pettibone would complain about me to the other teachers and if word would get to the judges about the troublemaker who had written a long paper just to annoy her teacher.

Mr. Pettibone collected the papers from the four students who were not competing for the Rattletop Award. All of them put together were shorter than the shortest Rattletop competitor. Mr. Pettibone nodded approvingly and put them on top of the stack. Then he gave us a lecture on the evils of competition in the classroom and how it perverts the educational process and gave us a reading assignment to do for the rest of the period while he started grading the papers.

"Whew!" Peter Mitchell said to me as we left the classroom at the end of the period. "If Pettibone didn't want to grade so many papers, why did he force everyone to write them? You didn't really write all that just to annoy him, did you?"

"Of course not," I said. "I just had so much information that it came out that way."

"Gee, I thought I had a lot about Neil Armstrong, but I barely made it to twenty-five pages. I thought a fat paper would get extra credit. I guess I was wrong." Peter looked sad. He must have wanted to win.

"How many footnotes did you have?" he asked.

"One hundred and twelve."

"That's a lot," Peter said. "I had twenty-four. I hope Pettibone doesn't mark me down for that."

I'd been so focused on the Rattletop Award, that I had completely forgotten that my research paper would also count toward my final grade in social studies. I had a straight A average, but I knew Mr. Pettibone didn't like me. And he'd been telling me all year that he didn't like me handing in assignments that were longer than what was required.

For the rest of the afternoon, I just counted the minutes waiting for classes to end. I'd been so proud of my research paper when I collected the carton from Greatgramps, and now, just a few hours later I wished I had never heard of Molly Pitcher.

When I got home from school, counting on Greatgramps to pull me out of my bad mood, he was in a mood that was worse than mine. I heard him on the telephone, and he was cussing up a storm. When he saw me, he lowered his voice and ended the conversation quickly.

"Who was that on the phone?" I asked. After serving two wartime tours in the Marine Corps, I knew Greatgramps must have plenty of swear words in his vocabulary, but I'd never heard him use them before.

"Mrs. Spinner," he said scowling. I wanted to laugh and then stopped. Greatgramps was serious. "She had a call from Mr. Pettibone," he said. "And so did I."

I knew Mr. Pettibone had called Mrs. Spinner to ask her to be a Rattletop judge, but why would he call Greatgramps? And what could he have said that would cause my perfect gentleman greatgrandfather to use a string of four letter words in conversation with a lady.

"Why would he call you?" I asked only the first question. "You've never even met him."

"Well it seems I am about to. He wants me to come over to the school for a conference. Says he'll be there all afternoon grading papers."

"Did he tell you why?" I gulped. I knew Mr. Pettibone was angry about my paper being so long, but that was no reason to go calling home about me.

"You don't need to know. I'm going over to the school, and Mrs. Spinner is going to meet me there. I'll tell you about it after I get Mr. Prissybone straightened out." Greatgramps stamped upstairs to his bedroom. "I'm going to wear my sanity hearing suit," he said.

"Can I do anything to help?" I said.

"Yes," he said, "you can. I want to borrow your box of Molly Pitcher notes. And let me have the yellow sheets you used for your rough draft."

I collected what Greatgramps asked for and handed it to him as he headed for the door. He didn't have to tell me; I'd figured out what must be going on. Mr. Pettibone thought that Mrs. Spinner had written my Molly Pitcher paper for me. I wanted to crawl into a hole and die.

twenty

Monmouth Battlefield

r. Pettibone gave me a B minus on my research paper because I wrote about several women instead of focusing on a single American hero. The Rattletop Committee had a better opinion of my work. I won the Rattletop Award.

Mr. Pettibone announced my name and called me to the stage at graduation. I had to shake his hand. Then I shook hands with the school principal, the members of the school board, the mayor and a lot of other people who were smiling and congratulating me. My hand still felt dirty from Mr. Pettibone's damp handshake.

Mom took the day off to come to graduation and Mrs. Spinner sat next to her with Greatgramps on the aisle. All of them wore their dress up clothes and looked very happy. I wore a new dress Mom bought for me, a pretty one for parties rather than for funerals, and I tried to make my face match the dress when I joined them after the program ended.

We walked to the Lindwood Inn, the fanciest restaurant in town, where Greatgramps had made reservations for lunch. The lunch was a combination graduation and birthday party for me. I'd be turning thirteen next week, and in the fall I'd be going to a new school. I should have felt proud and grown up, but I just felt old.

At the restaurant a man wearing a tuxedo welcomed us at the door, talked to Greatgramps like he was an old friend, and escorted us to a table by a window overlooking Lindwood Lake.

"George used to bring me here when we were courting," Mrs. Spinner said with a sigh after we were seated. "That was during the war, you know, and meat was rationed. Sometimes even when we had the coupons, there was nothing to buy at the store. George would bring me here and order steaks." She sighed again. Like Greatgramps, Mrs. Spinner had happy memories of World War II although to me it sounded awful.

"Mike brought me here, too," Mom said. "After he came home from the Gulf and before he got so sick. We'd hire a baby sitter and come here on Saturday nights. That was when we were living over on Lakeview Avenue," she said to me. "Do you remember that little house with a sunroom?"

"Not really," I said.

"In a few years you'll have a young man escorting you here," Greatgramps said.

I didn't think that was likely, although I didn't want to start an argument. Lakewood Inn was a nice restaurant, but young people didn't come here. Not to mention the problem of finding a young man who'd be interested in a weird girl. I buttered a piece of the crusty bread that came in a basket on the table and nibbled my salad.

"The food's good," I said. The others made appreciative sounds agreeing with me and we ate in silence for a while.

"Peggy," Mrs. Spinner said. "Do you miss Molly Pitcher?"

Mom laughed. "It does seem like we had another person living with us all year. Since Peg started working on that report, we heard more about Molly Pitcher than about any of her friends from school."

I didn't have any friends at school. And Mrs. Spinner was right. I did miss Molly Pitcher.

"How did you know?" I asked. I'd tried not to let anyone know how let down I'd been feeling the past few weeks. It wasn't just Mr. Pettibone being a jerk. That hurt, but what was worse was not having Molly in my head anymore. Tracking down evidence about her and building a case had been exciting. Now everything seemed boring.

"I feel the same way whenever I finish a book," Mrs. Spinner said. "I've come to love my characters and then, suddenly, they're gone. They're trapped between book covers where I can't change them anymore. Then it seems like there is nothing worth doing."

"How do you get over it?" I asked.

"I can answer that," said Greatgramps. "She starts another book."

"It's not quite that easy, Pat," Mrs. Spinner said. "First I have to find a way to say goodbye."

"How do you do that?" I asked.

"Well, when I finished *Mistress of Monticello*, I made a trip to Charlottesville, Virginia. I went to Monticello and walked around. Everyone who visits Monticello feels Jefferson's presence there, but I felt as if Sally Hemmings was there too even though I knew that the Sally I wrote about was ninety-nine percent fiction. So I said goodbye to Sally on that trip."

"And then she came home to, who was it?" Greatgramps asked. "Abigail Smith?" Mrs. Spinner nodded.

"I remember that book," I said excitedly. "It was *Goodwife of Quincy.*" Mrs. Spinner smiled.

"Mr. McAllister," she said to Greatgramps relaxing into her eighteenth century character. "Might I suggest that Miss Peggy be encouraged to make a visit to an appropriate venue to say farewell to Molly Pitcher?"

"What do you have in mind?" Greatgramps asked.

"That should be obvious, Mr. McAllister," Mrs. Spinner said. "I propose an expedition to Monmouth Battlefield."

And so on the last Saturday in June, Greatgramps, Mrs. Spinner and I got up before dawn, squeezed ourselves and a lunch basket into the sticker-mobile and headed up the New Jersey turnpike. Mom works on Saturdays. The idea of traveling for hours in what Mom calls Greatgramps's sardine tin to watch people dressed as colonial soldiers run around a hot field didn't appeal to her anyway.

"Do they do this reenactment every year?" I asked.

"I believe so," said Mrs. Spinner, "although in some years it's a bigger event than in others. I last visited in 1978, the bicentennial year, and the crowd was enormous."

"We'll be getting there early," Greatgramps said. "Just to be on the safe side, I made a call to an old friend who is into reenactments, reminded him that I was a World War II vet. He promised to make sure we get a good place to park and to watch the events."

"This is going to be a perfect day," I said happily. "I know it is."

And I was right. The day was sunny and hot, but we came prepared with sun lotion, hats, and plenty of water. Naturally, I thought a lot about water during the visit to Monmouth Battlefield State Park.

There were several creeks in the area where the great artillery battle was fought. One of them was Spotswood Middle Brook, which the Americans had to cross when they were retreating. There was another called Wamrock and another called Weamaconk.

There is a famous well, too, at Craig House, one of the buildings we visited on the tour. The interpreter told us a story about the Craigs. When they saw soldiers approaching they hid their silverware in the well and then abandoned the farm. During the battle, British soldiers were so thirsty they drank the well dry and found the Craigs's silverware at the bottom.

The question all the kids were asking was where Molly Pitcher had gotten the water she carried to the wounded soldiers. She might have carried water from a creek, but even if you didn't believe in the theory of coldwater disease, you wouldn't want to drink that. She couldn't have gone to the Craig House well because her husband's regiment, Proctor's Artillery, was all the way on the other side of the battlefield. Of course all the farms in the area had wells, more than one. People dug for drinking water in those days, and if a well went dry they'd dig for another.

A photograph in the book Greatgramps had given me for Christmas showed what the author called "the spring" from which Mary Hays had brought water. The photo isn't very clear except for two big signs on poles saying "Mollie Pitchers Well." A recent book about landmarks in women's history that I found in the library described what sounded like this well plus a real spring about 200 yards east of it; both claimed to be the "real" source of Molly Pitcher's water.

I didn't see how it mattered much where there was drinking water near Captain Proctor's artillery position that afternoon. Water wouldn't prove anything about a woman loading or firing a cannon. But I kept my mouth shut. I could tell that doubting the reality of Molly Pitcher would be an unpopular view among the tourists and interpreters at the site.

We went to the picnic area and spread out our lunch. Greatgramps was still showing off. He put a cloth tablecloth on the picnic table and set it with the Corningware dishes he keeps in the hamper. Then he brought out some real champagne glasses he found at the Salvation Army store and a bottle of sparkling cider. There was way too much food, but Greatgramps says that's the point of a picnic. After we'd had as much as we wanted, Greatgramps packed up the leftovers in the cooler. We took them back to the car and about 2:30 went to watch the reenactors line up to start the battle.

I really enjoyed this part. The battle reenactment lasted until 4:00, which was long enough for the spectators not to mention the people who had to play dead on the battlefield. The real battle had lasted for two and a half or three hours and was the longest battle of the war. After the battle reenactment there was another reenactment illustrating the activity of a field hospital and there were lots of women with buckets of water. I didn't see anyone with a pitcher.

By this time we were hungry again, so Greatgramps took out the cooler and we had supper. Then he spread a blanket on the grass. Mrs. Spinner and I lay next to each other listening to the sounds of tired children crying and tourists packing up and heading to their cars. The crowds were thinning and a breeze picked up bringing some welcome coolness. I felt well fed and perfectly content.

"I'm beginning a new book," Mrs. Spinner said dreamily as we watched the clouds drift by. "*Traitor in Petticoats* is finished and will be out for Christmas."

"Is that about the Lindwood loyalist's wife who was a friend of Peggy Shippen?" Greatgramps asked.

"Yes," Mrs. Spinner said. "That's the one."

"Was she real?" I asked. "Oh, probably not," Mrs. Spinner said. "But she could have been, and Peggy Shippen was real."

"Who is the heroine of the new book you are starting next?" I asked?

"She doesn't have a name yet," said Mrs. Spinner. "She might be Margaret or Mary or Molly. Or maybe Polly. A turning point in the story will be here at the battle of Monmouth."

"You're not writing about Molly Pitcher, are you?" Greatgramps said. "I've been through a year of her with Peggy, and I'd hoped for something different."

"Oh this will be different," Mrs. Spinner said. "The woman I am writing about was definitely not the Molly Pitcher Peggy was studying. Her husband will be infantry, not artillery, and the first battle she fights in is the Brandywine."

"The real Mary Hays story," I said excitedly.

"Maybe, or maybe not. Remember some people up in New York thought that Margaret Corbin had been at Brandywine. And they thought she'd been old enough at the time of the Revolution to have a grown son who was killed in the war along with her husband."

"So is this a Margaret Corbin story?" I asked.

"No, because we know Margaret Corbin was too young to have had a grown son, even a teenager." Mrs. Spinner watched the clouds and took a deep breath. My heroine is from the frontier area of Pennsylvania. She marries at seventeen and has her baby the next year. That makes her a bit over thirty when the action starts. Her husband joins up—maybe I'll call him John—and so does her son—I'll call him Johnny. My heroine is not about to stay home—I'll make her an orphan like Margaret Corbin—so she goes to war with her men. How do you like it so far, Peggy?"

"Super," I said. "Where's the love interest? It can't be her husband if he has to die. In your stories the hero and heroine always go off to live happily ever after."

"I haven't figured that out yet. Her husband dies at Monmouth..."

"She's the woman who takes her husband's place in line," I shouted, suddenly making the connection. "She's the one observed 'firing with all the regularity of a soldier.'"

"That's the kernel of truth in my plot," Mrs. Spinner admitted, "but I'm going to have her not just taking his place in this battle, but putting on his clothing and staying as a soldier in the army right through Yorktown."

"With a new lover," I added.

"Of course," Mrs. Spinner said.

"What's he like?" I asked.

"Ah, that is where the research comes in. He could be anyone or a combination of people."

"But gallant and handsome," I said.

"Someone like me," Greatgramps volunteered.

"Now that is an interesting possibility," Mrs. Spinner said.

"How are you going to do the research?" I asked.

"The usual way. Make up a list of things I'd like to know and then track down answers in books and manuscripts. The secret to writing good historical fiction is to have as many details as possible nailed down with footnotes."

"Like I tried to do with my Molly Pitcher project," I said. "I wish I had something as exciting as you have to spend time on this summer. I'm too young to get a job except maybe baby sitting, and I hate noisy little kids."

"I was thinking of hiring someone to assist me with my new book," Mrs. Spinner said smiling. "Someone to go to the library and order books though interlibrary loan, look things up in the indexes, and make xerox copies of the pages I need to study. I don't enjoy doing clerical work. That will give me more time to make up what fits in between the footnoted facts."

I cleared my throat. I couldn't believe what I thought she was saying. "Would you maybe consider a twelve year old, I mean a thirteen year old, as a helper?" I asked cautiously.

"Would you maybe be volunteering?" Mrs. Spinner asked laughing. She sat up and arranged her skirt.

"Mr. McAllister," she said. "Do be so kind as to pour some more of that lovely bubbly should there still be some properly chilled."

Greatgramps filled our glasses.

"I propose a toast," said Mrs. Spinner. "To Peggy, my new Inkling," she said. "And to next summer's Alicia Spinnaker novel, *Soldier in Petticoats*."

We clinked glasses, drank, and made our way from Monmouth battlefield.

"We'll come back next year," Mrs. Spinner said to me as Greatgramps turned the sticker-mobile onto the New Jersey Turnpike, "to say goodbye to ... Let me see," she said, her eyes twinkling. "I think I'll call my new heroine Peggy. Yes, we'll come back next year to say goodbye to Peggy Pitcher."

She settled back in her seat and closed her eyes. I knew she was already imagining details for the story she would write. I settled back and closed my eyes too as I imagined myself–and all the Molly Pitchers—having adventures in an Alicia Spinnaker romance. I knew for sure it was going to be a best seller.

CPSIA information can be obtained
at www.ICGtesting.com
Printed in the USA
BVOW03s0504160117
473201BV00005B/132/P